A MALIGNANT DEATH

Inspector James Given
Book Five

Charlie Garratt

SAPERE
BOOKS

A MALIGNANT DEATH

Published by Sapere Books.

20 Windermere Drive, Leeds, England, LS17 7UZ,
United Kingdom

saperebooks.com

ISBN: 978-1-80055-649-2

But now two mirrors of his princely semblance
Are crack'd in pieces by malignant Death.
— *Richard III*, William Shakespeare

PROLOGUE

The flickering bulb had bothered Ernest Parkes all week. He'd expected it to blow, so he'd be forced to do something about it, but it hadn't. If it had flashed constantly, he'd have taken the trouble to replace the damned thing. Instead, there'd be half an hour of steady illumination followed by two or three minutes of fitfulness. It wasn't as if there'd been the incentive of his machine being plunged into semi-darkness; the other factory lamps gave enough light. It was simply annoying.

Ernest was also convinced that it added to the headache he'd had every night recently. He knew it wasn't just the lightbulb, he had other things going on, but it didn't help. Tonight, it was worse than ever, and the engineer rubbed his forehead, leaving an oily smear. The argument he'd had in the late afternoon had brought this one on, he was sure.

Alone now on the factory floor, all the other workers having gone home for the night, it would be a chance to fetch the ladder and get the job done without twenty-five pairs of eyes watching. They were all good lads, but they'd not be able to stop themselves from barracking him, goading him into a slip or a mistake. No, this was better. Do it when they wouldn't see.

No longer a young man, Ernest had to rest twice as he carried the long wooden A-frame from the stores with the replacement bulb tucked safely in his overalls' pocket. He found the placement of the stepladder awkward because the errant lamp hung high above a lathe. Wrestling with the ladder forced another pause for breath.

Sitting there, he realised he hadn't often experienced the factory silent. All day long machines rattled, metal shrieked as it was torn, and the men's banter was endless as they pushed production forward.

When his breathing eased, Ernest realised the room wasn't entirely without sound, even now. An almost imperceptible electric hum. The momentary fizz of the faulty lightbulb. Waterpipes settling after a day's work. Together, the snoring of a sleeping workplace. And, somewhere upstairs in the offices, footsteps.

It took Ernest another minute to navigate the bank of switches to turn off the lights in his section, and another two to locate a glove so he'd not burn his hand. He'd never been comfortable with heights, and the stretch above his head to reach the bulb made his head spin. He grabbed the ladder, cursed, and counted to calm his breathing. When the panic passed Ernest squeezed his eyes shut, reached upwards again, and twisted the culprit from its bayonet.

With the defunct item in his pocket, he repeated the exercise with the new one. At full extension, with one hand on the shade and the other trying to feel the bulb into the fitting, a gasp escaped Ernest when the ladder rocked. This cry, for a split second, exploded to a scream as he fell.

Ernest heard the click of a door closing at the far end of the room. After this, only the sweet silence of eternal sleep.

ONE

Friday 14th June, 1940

My father had put down his scissors, stood, straightened his tie, wandered round the workshop, and pretended to look over the pieces created by his dozen cutters, trimmers and seamstresses. He moved along two rows of benches, one mounted with sewing machines, then to another large table beneath the tall window. Two men there inspected khaki trousers for flaws, before bundling them for despatch to army bases around the country. While winding this circuitous route, my father kept an eye in my direction, until he climbed the two steps to my desk for the fourth time that morning to ask about progress.

'Have you cheques for me to sign yet, Jacob? Are the invoices ready to go?'

'No, and I'll get nowhere if I have to stop every five minutes.'

He sucked sharply through his teeth. 'But these all need to be dealt with today. All of them.'

'And they will be, if you let me get on with it. Or would you prefer to look after them yourself?'

He'd rather do anything than deal with the accounts. Give him a needle and thread, a bolt of cloth, and a pattern, and he'd work from sunrise to sunset without complaint. This was why he'd bent over backwards to persuade me to take over some aspects of running the business when I returned from France. The problem was, he didn't trust me to do the job.

Despite my years away from home, he still thought of me as the impetuous sixteen-year-old who'd run away to sea.

'Why are they so urgent? You have plenty of orders, lots from the army. They pay straight away, and our suppliers are happy to wait because you've never let them down.'

'That's you all over, Jacob. You've never understood business. It's important to look after good customers and good suppliers alike. One sends us new orders, the other will look after us if there are shortages with this war. The name ... my name ... Dov Geffen, is respected, and we get the better service as a result than the man who holds back payment until the last minute. It's in our interest to keep them happy, and settle the paperwork as soon as we can.' He pulled his silver watch from his waistcoat pocket, stretching his arm to focus without his glasses. 'Look at the time, Jacob. I can't keep chatting here all day. Things to do.'

Having made it sound as if I was the one disturbing him, he turned to leave. I raised a finger and stopped him.

'Papa.'

'Jacob?'

'Could you, just once, call me James? James Given. It's my name now, and well you know it.'

'Not to me it isn't.'

And this is how it went. Every time. His continued use of my birth name, rather than the one I'd chosen for myself, symbolised how he saw me. To him, I'd always be a Russian Jewish boy and never an Englishman in his mid-thirties, with wife and a life, and at least as much experience of the world as he'd had. Even when I'd been a Detective Inspector, he'd always believed I'd see sense one day and become a tailor like him. I shook my head as he walked away.

Our house was flaming-June hot. Even in the kitchen at the back, with its cold, quarry-tiled floor and open window, the air was oppressive. I stood in the doorway, watching my wife as she washed lettuce at the sink, and wondered again, as I did most nights, how I could have married someone so beautiful. When we'd met less than a year earlier, I'd been knocked off my feet by this slim, witty, strong-minded woman who played piano, violin and cello like an angel, while I was of average height, overweight, and hardly a decent catch. But we got on well from the first moment and, even though she learned I found occasional solace in the bottle, we married within months.

I crossed the room to slip my arms round her waist from behind. She lay her head back on my shoulder.

'Mmm, that's nice. Good day?'

'Awful. Papa fussed the whole time. I wouldn't mind if his workshop was struggling, but it isn't. He has orders for weeks ahead, and even some from the War Office. From what I can see, his suppliers know he's a good payer, so why he was rushing to get the bills sorted out today I'll never understand. His biggest problem is getting the work done on time. With all the young ones conscripted, he's short of skilled men and there's so much competition for the retired ones to return.' I walked back to the doorway, wafting my face with my hat. 'To tell you the truth, I have to get away.'

'From your job?'

'And from here. I can't stand the city any longer.'

'But I thought you liked this house.'

I had no objection to the house, except that it was Rachel's and not ours. She'd owned it before we'd got together; it had been left to her from several owned by her father. Her brother, Bernard, got the rest. I'd sold my small cottage in Kenilworth after we married, reasoning that we could rent out her Birmingham home more easily when we left the country to start our new life in France. The Nazis put paid to that dream.

'It's not the house, it's the noise, and the smell of the city … and being crowded in all the time. I walk around and, unless I look straight up at the sky, all I can see are buildings. I didn't realise how much I'd miss our little place in Brittany.'

I'd worked on the French farm for a few months, and it had got into my bones and taken me back to when I was a young man working in the open air, sailing the world or picking fruit and sleeping under the stars. Rachel and I had prayed for France to hold back the Germans, hoping things would return to normal in a short time, but once the defences had been broken, we knew, as Jews, we needed to return to England.

Rachel began to carry our evening meal to the table. 'So what will we do?'

'I've been thinking about us buying a place in the countryside. Sell here, put the proceeds with the money I have left from my house, and try to find a cottage with some land. Enough to feed us and maybe produce left over for market. I could always get farm work again if we need it to make ends meet. What do you think?'

She rubbed her eyes. 'I don't know, James, it's all a bit sudden. We've only been back here five minutes. Let me finish serving tea, then we can chat while we eat.'

Rachel laid out our meals, then listened while I explained that it was something I'd considered even before we'd returned to Birmingham, and the feeling only grew stronger every time I left the house.

'I can't stay working with Papa for much longer. I'm not cut out for it, and he's driving me crackers. I want what we had in

Brittany. A cottage and some land to look after, except this time the land would be ours.'

'Have you anywhere in mind?'

'I have, actually.' I grinned and pulled a newspaper from my jacket pocket, flipping it open to where I'd marked two advertisements with my pen. 'These are in Kenilworth, and we're going to look at them tomorrow.'

Rachel looked at me, then at the newspaper, then at me again. 'Whoa, wait a minute. You've been planning to sell our house … my house … without discussing it with me?'

'Not planning, just thinking of options. I'm sorry. I thought you'd feel the same as me.'

Rachel shook her head. 'I'm not sure I do. I like the city. There are always people around, and it can be lonely out in the middle of nowhere. Anyway, that's not the point. You had no right to plan such a move before talking to me.'

I held up my hands. 'You're right. It was wrong of me.'

'It was, James, but you do it all the time. You seem to think you can snap your fingers and I'll follow. When we married, we agreed we'd both been independently single for so long that we couldn't face an unequal relationship.'

'Hang on. This isn't about equality —'

'Yes it is. If you believe you can plan our future without consulting me, then you must think you have a bigger say in it than I do.'

I stood, ready to escape to the front room and the wireless, but I stopped and sat again. Rachel was right. She and I had lived on our own for years before we'd met, and we'd both made our own choices in life. We hadn't yet been together long enough for the rough edges of that independence to have rubbed away, and we sometimes needed to take a step back from our opinions. Tonight, it was going to be my turn.

'I don't want to argue, Rachel. I've said I'm sorry, and I mean it. If I've been thoughtless, it was stupid of me. All I wanted was to do a little looking around without getting our hopes up. But, if you're unhappy, we can forget about the whole idea and just go to Kenilworth tomorrow as a day out, nothing more.'

Without speaking, Rachel cleared the table and washed the dishes. Usually, we'd chat while I put them away, but she was having none of it. She didn't speak to me for another two hours, until she made our bedtime Horlicks.

'I've been thinking about what you said, James, and I'm still not happy about what you did. But let me sleep on it. We can go on the trip, anyway. It will be nice to have a day out, and we'll see in the morning if I want to look at the houses.'

I opened my mouth to argue, but there was no point. My vision of our future would only work if Rachel wanted to go along with it. I washed the cups and put out the light, then followed my wife up to bed, where the atmosphere still hung with frost. I didn't fall asleep for a long time, and I suspected Rachel didn't either.

TWO

Saturday 15th June, 1940

Thunder in the early hours had brought a fresh breeze to the morning, which seemed to have blown away the tension between Rachel and me. With the sun shining, and the humidity gone, she'd agreed, over breakfast, we could add house-hunting to our trip after all.

I'd got rid of my car before we went to France. Petrol rationing, and living in the city and close to work, meant there was no point buying another, so I'd planned to take the train for our Saturday jaunt. Then I'd spotted a poster advertising a coach excursion to Kenilworth from the city centre.

I'd lived in Kenilworth for over ten years and I liked the town, which was small enough for its inhabitants to know one another. Though I'd seen bad things happen there during my career, and in the surrounding countryside, I'd loved my cottage by the castle, and I missed it sometimes. When our red and cream coach rattled to a halt outside Birmingham Town Hall, I was happy to climb on board. Though half the seats were taken by passengers who had boarded in Wolverhampton and the towns in between, we found a pair near the back, Rachel taking the one by the window. She had packed sandwiches and a flask of tea into a small haversack, which I swung onto my knee when we sat down. The other seats were soon filled by mothers, children and older couples in a holiday mood. It would be one of the few times in the year that any of them would leave the grey city streets. Across the aisle from us, a woman in her early twenties tried to settle her children — a boy in jacket, short pants and heavy shoes, and a curly-haired girl I assumed was his sister. Neither seemed to want to sit still, and the mother smiled apologetically to all her neighbours.

Once on our way, Rachel's face lit up as we passed through Warwickshire villages. From her seat by the window, she pointed to exuberant displays of roses and the neat vegetable plots. Fields shimmered after the overnight rain, lush and green before the harvest and, with the laughter and chatter of our fellow travellers, the world seemed at peace, even though it wasn't.

Rachel turned her attention away from the passing scenery. 'Hardly seems as if there's a war on, does it, James?'

'Not today. Not here.'

'But there is. Even France is about to surrender.'

I shrugged. 'Well, it was only a matter of time after Paris fell last week. They're saying Hitler is planning to humiliate the French by making them sign in Compiegne, where Germany signed after the last one.'

'Hardly seems right, does it, all the deaths over there, and we're on a charabanc trip?'

Rachel was right. Young men and women were being killed every day. God knew how many — the wireless didn't say — but our lives went on as normal. There was rationing and queues for food, and no cinemas or theatres, but, otherwise, we all went about our business in much the same way as we always did.

Rachel squeezed my hand. 'It's odd, isn't it? Children still come to me for their music lessons, you're still leaving the house for work every day, and the birds still sing in the skies above.'

'Well, I see some differences when I'm out and about. There's less traffic for one thing, and everyone seems to have an ear listening for the drone of bombers.'

'Do you think they'll come, James?'

'The wireless reports say it's inevitable.'

Rachel shivered, then leant over and stroked the handle of my walking stick hanging on the rail in front. For the first few weeks after we'd returned from Brittany, I'd drawn suspicious glances on the street, a seemingly fit man not in uniform. As a result, I'd taken to using a stick again, even when I didn't need it — a badge to show an injury kept me out of the army. Today, though, I'd need the stick for the miles we intended to wander round Kenilworth, looking for a new home.

'I'm so grateful you've not been called up. Small compensation for the pain, I know, but a blessing in these times.'

Now I squeezed *her* hand, and held it as the farms and hamlets slid by. In less than an hour, we reached our destination by the castle. We sat while the families in front filed off, then followed them into the sunshine.

'So what do we do first, James? This is your stomping ground.'

'One of the houses we want to see is on this side of town, about half a mile from here. We could go there first, and then come back to have our picnic by the castle. Afterwards, we can go up the hill and I'll pop into the police station to see who's about and say hello. The other place, the farm, is way out on the Leamington side. By the time we've seen it, we'll need to get back down here ready to go home. Is that all right with you?'

Rachel laughed. 'Sounds like you've got it all planned with military precision, so I'll just follow orders. Let's look at your old cottage first, though. It's only over the road.'

Nothing appeared to have changed since I'd moved out, other than there being a new coat of paint on the front door. I was tempted to knock but thought better of it. I didn't know the couple who'd moved in, and it might seem like prying. Instead, we just stood on the opposite pavement, arms linked, and looked for a minute or two before rambling away.

A quarter of an hour's walk down the road to Burton Green, we found the place we were looking for. It was stone-built and on a small junction, set back perhaps twenty feet. The front garden was packed with herbaceous flowers and shrubs, and roses grew over the arched gate.

Rachel smiled when she stepped through and took in the four windows with white frames. 'Very nice, and a similar size to the one in France. Love the garden.'

The owner, Mrs Harris, had advertised in the *Evening Gazette* and I'd sent a telegram to warn her we would call. A tiny lady of about sixty, wearing a cardigan and a floppy hat, answered my knock.

'Mr and Mrs Given? Please do come in. I'll make tea. You've walked a long way out to see me, and I'm glad of any visitors.'

Two cats wandered through from the kitchen and decided my trousers would be a good place to rub their heads. Our host poured three cups and invited us into the back garden.

Rachel stopped on the step and bit her bottom lip. 'Is there more land, Mrs Harris?'

'I'm afraid not, dear. Just my little lawn and a vegetable garden. We had the fields behind when my Dennis was alive, round about fifteen acres. I couldn't handle it on my own, and I sold it when he went. Did you want more?'

Rachel smiled and nodded. 'We did. I'm sorry we've wasted your time.'

'Ah well, it can't be helped. I should have been clearer in the advertisement, but the newspaper charges such a lot, you know.' Mrs Harris screwed up her eyes and peered at me. 'Do I know you, Mr Given?'

'Perhaps. I lived in the town for a good few years, down by the castle. I was in the police. You'll maybe have seen me about the place.'

'That will be it, I expect,' the old lady chuckled, 'not that I'd have much to do with the police.'

We chatted for a quarter of an hour over our tea. I explained we were looking for somewhere to grow enough to feed us, and perhaps keep a few animals. Mrs Harris said she didn't know of anywhere at present.

'If I hear of anything, I'll give you a call. I've got your number from your message. If you'd like me to, I could ask the farmer behind if he'd be willing to sell the field back?'

I said we'd be grateful if she would, then thanked her and left. Rachel spoke as soon as we were out of earshot.

'What did you think of it?'

'Very nice. I could see you loved the cottage.'

'I'd have jumped at it if she had more land.'

'Really?'

'Come on, James, you know *you* would. Perhaps Mrs Harris will convince her neighbour to sell back a couple of fields. That would give us a start, at least.'

By the time we arrived at the castle, I was ravenous. We wasted no time in finding a grassy spot below the red sandstone walls, where we were shielded from the breeze. I'd seen the spot used a hundred times from my gate. I wondered if someone was sitting at a window now, looking over and watching the day-trippers eating their lunch in the sunshine and gazing across the fields. At my desk by that window, I'd spent many an hour pondering, using the grass and the big sky to see beyond the bare facts of a case, hoping for an insight. Unusually, although the castle sat on a mound and had a view for miles in most directions, it lay on the edge of the town and was at the bottom of a hill. It had been a target for tourists like us since it went out of use after the Civil War.

A restless night, our morning walk, and the lunch of sandwiches and cheese packed by Rachel almost made me nod off, until the peace was shattered by three Spitfires roaring in formation overhead. The noise of their engines rattled off the castle wall, causing the cows grazing by a stream to stampede away.

Rachel squeezed my hand. 'Makes it real, doesn't it?'

'It's real enough anyway, don't you think? It's on every news item on the wireless, and it's all anyone talks about.'

'It is, but seeing those planes up close is different somehow. Almost like the war's right here, in our backyard.' She shivered. 'Anyway, I'll not rest now, so we might as well go on our way. You said you wanted to call in at the police station on the way?'

'Just to say hello if anyone is around. Do you mind?'

'Provided it's quick. I've not come out for the day to spend it in some stuffy police station.'

I promised I wouldn't be too long, and we began the climb up the hill to town, after I dropped our rucksack back in the coach. Halfway up, we turned into Abbey Fields and meandered past the lake to the other end then round to the police station. I suggested Rachel should go to a café for a cup of tea while I went inside. She told me she'd be annoyed if I kept her waiting and, knowing I'd only just got out of her bad books, I promised I'd be no more than quarter of an hour.

I stood for a couple of minutes across the road from the police station, the flagpole distinguishing it as an official building, unlike its neighbours. Looking up at my old office, remembering the horrors of my last cases, I wasn't sure if going inside would be such a good idea, but curiosity propelled me across and up the two steps. At the front desk was Sergeant Tommy Burns, who threw his hands in the air and clapped as soon as he looked up from his paperwork.

'Inspector, how good to see you. Checking up on us, are you?'

Burns would now be close to retirement, having spent many a good year dealing with concerned members of the public, and processing villains brought in by his colleagues. I'd never been sure if he'd been chosen for the job because he looked like a desk sergeant, or if he'd physically developed to fill the position. His sedentary days spent at the desk had done nothing to constrain his waistline, and his wide smile shining through half-moon spectacles was guaranteed to put visitors at ease. We'd usually got on well, particularly as I rose up the ranks and showed I was a decent detective, as committed as Burns was to keeping the town safe.

'It's just James now, Tommy. You're well, I hope?'

'Never better.' He looked at my stick. 'Your leg still not right?'

'Good days and bad days. We're in town to look at some houses, so we have a couple of long walks today. I thought I'd need it.'

'You're thinking of moving back to Kenilworth? I thought you had your sights set on foreign parts.'

'I did, and it's a long story. We're in Birmingham at the minute, but I want to get out. Is anyone about?'

'Afraid not. Well, no-one you'd know anyway. Saturday, always quiet, and a few of the younger ones have joined the forces even though they don't need to.' Burns rapped his knuckles on his desk. 'Hang on. Phil Trimble called in. He might still be upstairs. I'll give him a buzz.'

Inspector Phil Trimble and I had been colleagues, and he'd taken over my job after I'd left, but I wouldn't have said we were friends. He'd been a bit of a plodder and sometimes too willing to take the easiest explanation at face value. He'd also been a bit too openly religious for my liking, always ready with a spoken prayer or a bowed head if he thought the occasion warranted it. Within a couple of minutes I heard shoes coming down the stairs, and Phil turned into the reception area wearing a broad but polite smile. He had on a green tweed jacket and held a manilla folder under his arm.

'James, what a surprise.' He shook my hand. 'You've been in France, I hear.'

'For a few months, yes. Became a little too hot after the invasion, so we're back.'

Trimble glanced at his watch. 'Actually, James, I don't really have much time today. I only came in to pick up these papers. Can we catch up another day?'

'It's fine, Phil. My wife and I are only in Kenilworth for a few hours, a bit of an excursion, but I may be here again in the not too distant future. I'll give you a call and we can perhaps grab a bite to eat.'

'That would be great. I'm sorry, but I do have to dash.' He glanced at the desk sergeant. 'Give James a cuppa, Tommy. Make him feel at home.' My successor waved with his folder and headed out of the door.

'Don't bother with the tea, Tommy. I've not much time myself. Told Rachel I wouldn't be long.'

We chatted for a few minutes about who was still at the station, who'd moved on or been promoted, and who'd left. Tommy avoided any mention of the constable who'd been my partner on my last case before I'd left, someone he'd grieved for almost as much as I had. I asked if he'd heard from our old boss, Superintendent Dyer.

'Still not got away to the seaside — some kind of problem selling his house. The war, I expect. Sure you won't have that tea? I'm having one myself.'

I refused again, and told him I had to be off. 'Good talking to you, Tommy. Give my regards to the lads and tell them I'm sorry I missed them. Maybe next time.'

I left and hurried round to the café to meet Rachel. Through the plate glass window, I could see she was still drinking tea, and engaged in conversation with a woman with a baby on the next table. I waited for a couple of minutes to catch her eye, and then had the satisfaction of tapping on the glass and holding up my watch to suggest she was now keeping me waiting. Her frown disappeared when she saw me chuckling on the street. It didn't stop her folding her arms, shaking her head and mouthing the word "idiot" at me, before paying her bill and joining me.

The farm turned out to be no good. It was far too big and very run down, with a strong smell of animals and black mould growing on the bedroom walls. The half mile walk out there had been a waste of energy. At least it meant we were back in good time for our motor-coach, and I was glad to sit down for a while.

The other passengers returned in dribs and drabs, some of the men garrulous and flushed from spending the afternoon in the pub, the children red-faced from running about in the sun for too long. Everyone seemed to be in good spirits, and we'd barely pulled away from the castle when the singing started. It continued until we reached the suburbs of Birmingham.

In the lull, I asked Rachel if she'd enjoyed her day.

'It was lovely. Tiring, but lovely. Kenilworth is so nice.'

'You remember when we bumped into each other that day outside the castle, only the second time we'd met?'

She smiled. 'I do.'

We'd met in Birmingham while I was trying to find Meena, the German Jewish refugee my parents took in before the war started. The girl went missing and Rachel had been her violin teacher. She hadn't known where Meena had gone, but I'd been very taken with Rachel's stunning looks and sense of humour, so I was glad to have bumped in to her later, only a few steps from my front door. Even though I'd been busy, I'd dropped almost everything to spend the day sightseeing with her.

A baby at the front of the bus wailed, and everyone peered to see what was going on. A couple of the older women tutted and shook their heads, as if no child of theirs would ever make such a racket. I took Rachel's hand.

'So would you consider moving to Kenilworth?'

She laughed. 'James, you are relentless. Isn't it enough I let you take me out there today? Doesn't it tell you I'm not completely set against the idea? It's just such a big step — plus you sprung it on me without any discussion. Perhaps if you'd thought about it properly, you'd have brought me on the trip first, then suggested we might move. That would have been the clever way to play your hand.'

When I'd played cards, unless I was drunk, I'd been a shrewd gambler, never looking for the quick win, but luring my opponent into a false sense of security. Rachel was right — I'd been clumsy. My excuse was that I'd assumed she'd have been as keen to leave the city as I was. The fact she was still talking to me suggested I shouldn't lose hope.

'You will think about it, then?'

'I suppose I'll have to — you seem so keen. But don't keep going on about it. Let it simmer for a few days, and we'll see what comes out the other end.'

A few minutes before we arrived back in Birmingham, Rachel took my hand. 'I'm not promising anything, James, but I did love Mrs Harris's cottage. I could see myself there if she can convince her neighbour to sell back some of the land.'

Half an hour later, I still had a smile on my face and we were home. A telegram lay on the mat behind the front door. I picked it up and ripped open the envelope. 'How strange.'

Rachel filled the kettle. 'What's that, James?'

'It's from Henry Dyer. I was just asking about him earlier.'

'Is there something wrong?'

'Hard to tell. He's asked if I can visit him in Leamington. Says he's a favour to ask but can't go into it in a telegram.'

'What will you do?'

'Well, I can't drop everything and go over there. My father would go mad. I'll send a note back in the morning and tell him it will need to wait until next weekend.'

THREE

Friday 21st June, 1940

My father closed the workshop at three o'clock on Friday afternoon, as he always did, winter or summer, to be sure he and his workers would be home ready for sunset and Sabbath.

The building had three storeys, plus a cellar where the cloth was stored. The working area, where all the tailoring was done, had high windows to let in the light, a double door at the front for loading, and two tables at the back, where the men and women took their meals.

Before heading off for the weekend I followed him through a door in the corner, and up the stairs to the family's rooms on the two upper floors. Close behind, Anna, my cousin, and Meena followed, both now working for my father and staying in his home. A home which was becoming increasingly crowded even though my brother, Eli, had joined the army and left a room spare.

When Uncle Gideon had died, Anna and her mother, my Aunt Miriam, had fled France, taking sanctuary with my parents and joining their refugee Kindertransport guest. With my younger sister, Sarah, and my mother, there were now five women under Papa's wing. He confessed he regularly took sanctuary in the parlour, unable to face their presence every evening.

Even though it was the middle of summer and not due to be dark for several hours, my mother and sister were busy preparing food for the evening meal. Mama wiped her hands on a towel and hugged me.

'James, you've come to join us? Is Rachel with you?'

'I'm sorry, not tonight. I have to go to Leamington for a couple of days, so I thought I'd come and see you before I go. Rachel may call round on Sunday, if you'll be home.'

'Where would I go? Tell her she's more than welcome to join us for lunch.' Mama glanced round the room and shrugged. 'One more isn't going to make any difference. It will be nice to have a chat without you always at her side.'

'It's good to know how popular I am.'

'You know that's not what I mean, James. It is good to see you any time.'

I laughed. 'I know, Mama. I was only joking.'

My father made his excuses and went to change, and the five of us chatted for a few minutes before I said I must leave. I told my mother I'd be back by Monday, then wandered home in the sunshine to get ready for my trip.

An hour later, I was standing on the long central platform of Moor Street station when the green engine sighed to a stop, filling the air with steam. Passengers poured off the brown and cream carriages, to be replaced by crowds of new travellers searching for the best seats. Commercial salesmen, shop-girls, families with small children, all heading out of the city for the weekend, or forever. Most packed themselves into third-class, so I had no trouble finding a seat by the window in a second-class compartment. I settled back with my newspaper, waiting for the final doors to slam and the parting whistle to shriek.

On the bench opposite, two elderly ladies, who I judged to be sisters by their matching check outfits, started a whispered conversation as we pulled away, then lifted out wool and needles from the cavernous matching handbags they had on their laps. The click-clack of their needles seemed strangely in time with the wheels on the tracks, and with each other. A gentleman on my side of the bench, dressed in a camel-coloured suit and waistcoat, as well as a yellow cravat, looked up from his book, smiled at the women, then returned to his reading.

I alternated between reading my newspaper and looking out of the window, across summer fields, some with cattle, others with crops, making me think of my friends in Brittany. The paper, full of stories of the progress of the war, carried a report on the hardships being visited on the French since the German invasion, particularly in the north, where it was now under Nazi administration. The occupying army had commandeered food supplies, so times would become difficult, particularly for citizens of towns, where they had no opportunity to grow produce of their own.

The view reminded me how beautiful England was outside of the cities, and how similar it was to France with its fields and farms. I could see the people I'd known in Vieux-Croix going about their business, but no longer free. It was frightening to think that only twenty-two miles of water separated England from the same fate.

The train journey took only a little over half an hour, and we were trundling into Leamington station before I had time to dwell on this too much. The knitters packed away their handiwork and our companion stood, lifted a small case from the shelf above his head, and put his book away, after turning over a page corner. Passengers blocked the corridor, so we couldn't leave the compartment straight away, and he spoke to me for the first time.

'Just down for the weekend, y'know. Visiting my sister and her husband. Bit of a break. He moved over here for work — some kind of engineering job, I think. You?'

I stood and dropped in behind him in the queue shuffling towards the doors. 'I'm only here for a couple of days too. Just staying with a friend.' We stepped down onto the platform and I pointed towards the footbridge. 'I'm heading over there. Nice talking to you.' Without waiting for a reply, I made my way out of the station, walking in the direction of the river. I found Henry Dyer's house, which was impressively tall and broad, like the man himself. It was a double-fronted, three-storey residence surrounded by mature rhododendrons, like a dozen neighbouring houses facing a park, though it commanded the corner site overlooking the town's bowling green. Inside the gate, the garden path led past rose beds, and perhaps the best cut lawn I'd ever seen, to two steps and the front door. There was a rumour that Mrs Dyer's family had money, and I was sure the couple would not be able to afford a place like this on a superintendent's salary. I knocked and my ex-boss's silhouette appeared on the other side of the stained-glass panel.

'James!' He stuck out his hand. 'Come in.' The tiled hall, hung on one side with landscapes, and on the other with portraits, led to a large kitchen, where a yapping Jack Russell terrier tugged at my trousers. Dyer picked up the dog and scratched it behind the ears. 'This is Ben. A naughty little man.'

A tall, slim woman, dressed in a grey check dress with a black velvet collar and cuffs, stood with her back to the sink, her brown, curled hair highlighted by the sun streaming through a substantial window.

Dyer walked over and put his arm around her tiny waist, his bulk dwarfing her in the process. She looked at least ten years his junior. He'd let himself go to seed and she clearly hadn't. 'This is Audrey. I don't think you've met.'

'Not properly, sir,' I said, reaching out to shake her hand. 'Though I've seen you together at force dinners.'

'Ah, of course. But you must stop that "sir" nonsense. That's all behind us, and I can't have you staying in my house unless we're on first-name terms. Just wouldn't do. What do you say, Audrey?'

Audrey smiled and shook my hand — a limp and polite gesture, suggesting she had better things to think about than her husband's social niceties. 'I'm sure you and Mr Given will work out the right thing, dear. Now, I need to nip down the road to pick up some final things for dinner. The two of you take a drink outside and I'll be back in no time.'

She lifted a shopping basket from the table, nodded in my direction, and left us to our own devices.

'You must pardon my wife, James. She's not usually so offhand. Tomorrow would have been Sarah's birthday, and it's been playing on Audrey's mind.' Sarah, their daughter, had been knocked down by a drunken driver when she was seventeen. 'She'd have been thirty-five.'

'I'm sorry, sir … Henry.'

'She'd probably have a family of her own by now.' He shuddered. 'Still, mustn't dwell, eh? Now, can I get you that drink?'

I told him I'd just take a glass of cordial if he had one.

'Still not drinking, then. That's good. Wish I'd the willpower.'

He knew as well as I did that it wasn't willpower, it was necessity. One drink would lead to another, then another, and I'd been down that road too many times. If I wanted to keep my self-respect and my wife, it was easier to stick with soft drinks.

My host poured mine then splashed a good shot of whisky from a crystal decanter into a long glass with the merest dash of water, and asked me to open the kitchen door out to the garden. Dyer nodded towards the shade of a red-leaved tree, where he placed the two glasses on a table, then sat at one end of a bench, waving for me to take the other. The lawn at the rear of the house was as well trimmed as at the front, except for a few square yards at one end which appeared to have been recently dug.

'It really is good of you to come over, James.'

'I'm happy to, if there's something you think I can help with. You did enough for me in your time.'

'That's decent of you to say. Just doing my job, you know. Not many coppers about with your talents, James — I could see it when you first joined us. Any assistance I gave was paid back a hundred times with your success rate.' He leaned back against the bench and pulled on an earlobe. 'It's funny, this retirement.' He lifted a gold watch from his waistcoat pocket and dangled it on its chain, then leant across and showed me the inscription on the back.

'They gave me this when I left. Now I've all the time in the world, but I can't get excited about anything. I had it all planned out. We'd sell up here, move to the coast, and I'd spend some time getting our new home nice.' He patted his stomach and smiled. 'Then I'd lose a few pounds and concentrate on getting down my golf handicap. The war's put paid to all that. The house sale is held up, the golf course is closed for the duration, and Audrey's already fed-up with me under her feet. That's why I've begun digging a vegetable garden, despite planning to move. God knows how long we'll be stuck before we can. They say the rationing will be extended before too long, so if I grow a few spuds and cabbages it should help out. Poor Audrey is scared half to death there will be no food in the shops before long, so it makes sense for me to try to grow some of our own. What do you think?'

'I'd say it's a good idea. Rachel's been trying the same at home. You're not happy, then?'

'Don't get me wrong, I couldn't have stayed in the force for much longer, and I keep busy. I've taken up bowls across the road there, I've joined a chess club, and I get out to the golf clubhouse for a pint in the evenings. I take the dog for a trot every morning, and I walk into town with Audrey most days, or along the river, but it's not the same as going out to do a proper job every day, is it?'

I'd never thought of retirement in those terms. I supposed I'd assumed it would be one long holiday. Even though I'd finished in the police about the same time as my boss, I hadn't retired — I'd moved to France almost straight away and begun working on Malo Legrand's farm. When I'd come back, I'd immediately started in my father's workshop. I wasn't destitute but still needed some money coming in.

'So, with all this time on your hands, Henry, what did you want me to do for you?'

'Not really a matter of your time, James — it's your skill. I was at a desk for far too long to tackle investigations any longer.'

'It's an investigation?'

'In a manner of speaking. There's a man I met at the golf club; he runs an engineering firm here in the town. We've become friends, and he's told me he has a bit of a problem which he doesn't want to bother the police with. He asked if I could help but, as I said, I'm not sure I could manage it any longer.'

'And you think I can?'

Henry laughed. 'I know you can, James. Sharpest detective I ever managed. Never knew how you did it, always seeing the small details others missed.'

I was about to dismiss his flattery when the kitchen door opened and Audrey Dyer popped out her head. 'I'm back, gentlemen. Dinner in fifteen minutes. Henry, have you shown your friend his room? Give him chance to freshen up before we eat.'

Henry stood, clearly used to following his wife's orders. He collected the glasses and waved for me to follow him inside. 'We'll go down to the clubhouse to meet my friend later, and he can explain everything. If you think it's too much trouble, just say and I'll tell him to talk to the local boys after all.'

Upstairs, Henry led me to a large bedroom, then whistled away down the landing. Net curtains fluttered in the draught, and I went over to the bay window to look out. A young man with an empty shirt sleeve pinned to his chest, and a boy I thought must be his son, kicked a football across the grass in the park opposite. A little further away, eight older men in white trousers and shirts played bowls on the green. Swallows swooped and darted above the river beyond a line of trees, taking flies in the warm evening air.

A gong sounded from the hall below and Henry shouted a reminder that I had five minutes. A splash with soap and water, a quick change into a clean shirt, and I was downstairs without being called a second time. The meal smelled delicious — roast chicken, buttered new potatoes and a salad.

We ate slowly, exchanging stories about our experiences in the force, and Henry's in the army before that. Audrey chipped in with her own observations, reminding her husband when he appeared to be exaggerating or misremembering. She turned out to be an amusing and good-humoured hostess once she'd relaxed in my company.

When we'd finished, Henry called his dog over, who'd been eyeing us from a basket in the corner of the room, and dropped a few chicken scraps on the floor. The Jack Russell wolfed them down and looked up for more. Henry lifted Ben onto his knee and scratched the dog's head.

'We nearly lost him a few weeks ago, you know.'

'How?'

'Went out in the garden at night like he usually does, then we went to bed. Next morning, he'd been sick all over the kitchen and was lying limp in his basket. Got him to the vet, who said it must have been something he'd eaten.' Henry glanced at his wife, who appeared to give the slightest shake of her head. 'I think he'd been poisoned, but Audrey doesn't agree.'

She shivered. 'It's just too awful to contemplate, don't you think, James? Who would want to kill our poor little dog? I think he might just have nibbled on a plant he shouldn't have — there are plenty in the garden which can do harm. Not many people realise that.'

Audrey didn't need to tell me this. Only a year earlier, I'd almost been the victim of someone's expertise in toxic flowers. I shivered at the thought before Henry cut back in.

'My lovely wife might be right. I can't seriously think anyone would want to do our dog, or us, any harm. It does make you wonder, though, doesn't it?' With this, Henry stood and began to clear the table. 'We'd best be on our way, James. I said we'd be with my friend by eight and it's almost that now.'

By the time we'd left the house and climbed into Henry's five-year-old Austin Seven, the sun had sunk behind an evening heat haze, and the stillness of the air suggested a thunderstorm might be on its way. Henry wound down a window as we pulled off his drive.

'Damned warm, James. I expect I'll not get much sleep tonight — not without a couple of pints in any case.'

34

We drove alongside the park and I looked at the people out for a stroll, many of the women fanning themselves to try to keep cool. Children of all ages ran around on the grass, despite the heat, and one group of boys even engaged in an impromptu game of football, though I guessed they'd have moved a little more quickly had it been ten degrees colder.

We drove past grand, white houses with black-painted verandas, then smaller, terraced, brick-built homes occupied by the better off workers and professionals of the town. Soon, even these thinned, and we were out in the open countryside. A few minutes took us the half mile or so to the golf course — vast, manicured fields devoid of players, and notices declaring the course was closed due to wartime restrictions. Henry navigated off the main road, through large iron gates, and pulled up outside a Georgian country house with "Leamington Golf Club" picked out in gold lettering on a wooden board on the wall by the door.

The clubhouse sang of exclusivity. Wood panels on two walls, red, plush carpet everywhere, and subtly displayed notices reminding members what they could, and could not, do on the premises. When we walked inside, four men occupied one table. A man on his own, in a grey check suit which looked like it would cost me a few week's wages, sat at another, overlooking the fenced-off final green. He stood and raised a hand.

'Henry. Over here.' He was six foot, with thick, greying hair. He was possibly a year or two older than Henry, but fitter and muscled. He shook Dyer's hand and introduced himself as Alec Kendrick. 'And this must be your Mr Given. What can I get you both?'

My old boss initially asked for a whisky and dry ginger, but changed to a pint of bitter, saying he'd a thirst. I ordered a lemonade, marking me down straight away as either an ex-alcoholic or a prude. I let Kendrick decide which version of me he preferred. When he returned with the drinks, the men chatted for a minute or two about how they were missing playing and hoping that the course would be allowed to re-open soon. Dyer, as he often did, adopted the optimistic approach.

'At least we're safe and not being shot at, Alec. Plenty of young lads, some of them my ex-colleagues, are on the other side of the Channel facing German tanks.'

Kendrick stroked his chin. 'I suppose you're right. Still, we had our share in the last lot. Can't see the sense in stopping our golf, though. Not like the bombers are hovering over Leamington waiting to target us.' He laughed, knocked back half of his pint, and turned to me. 'Anyway, we'd best get down to business. Tell me something of yourself, Mr Given.'

'What sort of thing?'

'Your police experience, for example.'

'Why?'

I knew Kendrick ran a factory, and was used to giving instructions and having them obeyed. I didn't want him to gain the impression he could do the same with me. Henry shot me a look across the table. 'Now, James, don't be awkward.'

I gritted my teeth and gave Kendrick the minimum. 'Twelve years' service, all of it under your friend. Finished last year as Detective Inspector.'

'Bit young to retire, aren't you?'

'I was wounded. Stabbed in the thigh. Didn't fancy spending the rest of my days at a desk filing old case records. So I left.'

'Henry says you were a good detective. Thorough.'

'That's nice of him.'

'Are you discreet?'

'I can be.' I looked at my watch. 'Where's this going, Mr Kendrick? Henry told me you needed some help. I didn't expect the third degree.'

Kendrick sat back in his seat and took another sip from his glass. 'I'm sorry, Mr Given. I can be a bit direct sometimes. The manager in me, I suppose. It's just that I need to be sure I'm doing the right thing, and that you're up to the job.'

'You're now making it sound very clandestine.'

He laughed — an easy, relaxed, laugh. 'Well, I expect it is, in a way, but isn't all detective work? It's not top secret, though. I'm not recruiting you into a spy network.'

The man didn't know I'd already been down that road and experienced how military intelligence recruitment worked. 'Then please get to the point, Mr Kendrick.'

'I hope it's quite straightforward, really. Henry will have told you I run an engineering firm here in Leamington?'

'Yes.'

'It's not a big outfit, and most of our work is for the car manufacturers in Coventry.'

'You're the owner?'

'No, I'm not. We were set up by my father and he's still alive, so, technically, he's in charge.'

Kendrick paused and Henry intervened. 'The old boy is almost ninety and not in the best of health, so, to all intents and purposes, Alec is the boss, James. He's just being modest.'

'Henry's good to give me such credit and it's true Dad's not involved much anymore, but his name is over the door. I manage the company on his behalf. As I say, we largely make components for motor car manufacturers where they don't have the capacity or specialism to do it themselves. Usually, there's nothing exciting about what we do. Cogs, gears, spindles, that kind of thing. All of them have switched to war work now, and one of our long-standing customers is involved in the aeroplane engine business. As you can imagine, they're going flat out to get a step ahead of Germany. As a result, they've asked some of our designers to lend a hand, and this is where you come in.'

I shrugged. 'But I know nothing about engineering.'

Another laugh. 'No, no, I'm not making myself clear. If we can get this to work, it's a very big step up for us with the war on. Our usual business is down, but the big factories need to make more. We've stepped up to working six days a week because small firms like ours need to show we're able.' His face became serious. 'It's been going well, but now some of our designs seem to have gone astray.'

'You mean they've been stolen?'

'Not exactly. One or two weren't there when the designer looked for them early one morning, then they showed up later where they should have been. Almost as if they'd been borrowed. It has happened a few times since.'

'I'm sorry, Mr Kendrick. I still don't understand. If the designs have just been mislaid for a while, where's the harm?'

'Engineering, particularly at this cutting edge, is small steps. People think things are invented fully-formed, but that's not the case. Someone has an idea, then someone else tinkers with a prototype. After that, another engineer might shave a thousandth of an inch off a component, or add an extra cog, and get a big increase in efficiency. This goes on, in increments, until the right materials are found and the cost is affordable enough for it to go into production and on to the market. Even then, changes are made to the design all the time to make it cheaper, better, easier to produce and so on. You only have to compare aeroplanes in the last war with those in this one to see what I'm getting at.'

'So you're saying if another company gets its hands on your idea and improves on it, or gets it to market before you do, they'll have an advantage in stealing your customers?'

'Precisely, Mr Given.'

'So why haven't you called in the police?'

'There's a very small team involved with this particular job, all good men, and I don't want the police tramping around in their size-nines upsetting them. I hate to think one of our chaps is involved, but I can't see who else it might be.' Kendrick paused and bit his top lip. 'And there's another slight complication.'

'What is it?'

'One of the team was killed last month. An accident. Fell off a ladder. The problem stopped for a couple of weeks after Ernest Parkes died, but now it's started again. I thought he'd been the one.'

'So why is this a "complication", as you put it?'

'When the police came round to check the circumstances of Ernest's death, I didn't mention the missing drawings. The whole affair would have become public knowledge, and I can't chance people thinking we're not secure; it would put a complete block on us getting this kind of work. It would be a great help if you could take a look, discreetly, then let me handle the culprit if you can find him.'

Dyer stood up. 'There you have it, James. Should be a piece of cake for a man of your abilities. Let me get another drink in while you think about it.'

I was glad of the opportunity to avoid replying. The last thing I wanted was to go back to being a policeman, especially an unpaid one. I'd had enough difficulties in France trying to investigate a case with no official status. I confirmed I'd have another lemonade and, when he'd gone, I turned the conversation to general questions about Kendrick's company. He told me his father had worked as a boy on the railways, showing a bent for machines, and landed alongside an engineer, where he learned many of the skills which would lead him to set up his own company at the turn of the century. He'd had very little formal education, so he'd engaged people who knew their way around sales and bookkeeping. Within ten years, he'd built up a fine business and a reputation for good work at a good price. The old man had continued running the firm on a daily basis until well after normal retirement, then kept his hand in for a while. It was only ten years earlier that he'd succumbed to old age, and Alec had needed to take over completely.

When he returned from the bar, Dyer placed my lemonade in front of me. 'Now, James, have you agreed to help Alec?'

'I'm afraid I need to give it more thought. If the factory is now working on Saturday, I can call in tomorrow and make a start, but if I'm to spend more time over here, I'll need to talk to my wife and my father.'

Kendrick frowned. 'Your father? What's he got to do with it?'

'I work for him. If I want time off, we'll have to agree when I can make it up. I'm sure you can understand that.'

Kendrick clasped his hands under his chin and nodded. 'Of course I can, Mr Given. Give me the time you can spare and then just have a think about it and talk to your family. Let me know in a day or two if you're able to do anything more and if not, so be it. I'll need to find someone else.'

FOUR

Saturday 22nd June, 1940

In the week before coming to Leamington, I'd pressed Rachel over and over about what she'd said on the coach on our journey home from our excursion. On Sunday and Monday she'd batted it away, telling me to give her time to think, but by Wednesday evening we'd begun to have a serious discussion about what we might both be looking for in a new home, and how we might afford it. We had decent savings, propped up largely by the cash from the sale of my house, which we'd not needed to raid during our time in France. Rachel was certain her brother, Bernard, would dip into his considerable pockets if she asked, and there was always the possibility of renting somewhere if we couldn't manage to buy outright. It seemed unlikely we'd be able to sell Rachel's house; the war and the start of a German bombing campaign on cities had put paid to any chance of that for the foreseeable future. In some ways this was an advantage, because renting it out would provide us with a steady income until we were established in our new location.

We were agreed on most things we wanted in a home. I had more of an eye on the size and quality of the land we needed, whereas Rachel considered proximity to town more of a priority, so she'd be able to attract music students. We made lists and then scoured the newspapers during the week, finding three properties of possible interest within a mile of Leamington centre which I could look at.

We'd made sure the properties were on the same side of town, so I wouldn't have to walk too far, but Henry offered me a lift on the Saturday morning.

'Least I can do, James,' he said, though I suspected his generosity had less to do with my welfare than with him wanting me to spend as much time as possible on Kendrick's problem.

The storm promised the previous night hadn't arrived and it was still sticky and unpleasant, even with the car windows open, so I was pleased not to be cooped up for too long. The first house was so tumbledown it would have taken a fortune to make it anywhere near habitable. The second lay between a sewage farm and a commercial piggery, which we smelled before we saw. This had conveniently been ignored in the advertisement. We drove by without stopping.

An elderly man in a brown cardigan opened the door to the final place, a rambling cottage which had been extended over many decades. He introduced himself as Albert Perkins, tapped his walking stick on the floor, and pointed at mine.

'The war?'

'No, afraid not. Injured at work.'

'Hmm, mine's just old age. Used to run the mile for the county harriers and can't even walk around this place now. That's why I'm selling up. Come in, have a look around.'

I followed him into a hallway leading to a low-ceilinged living room. Cosy but in need of some decoration. A wood stove against one wall burned, and I wondered how thin his blood must be to need a fire and extra layers of clothing in mid-summer. There were three decent bedrooms, one full of junk, and a large kitchen with a pantry. Mr Perkins led me through a door in the corner of the kitchen to a recently-built room, with windows overlooking the garden. The walls were not plastered, and the woodwork was unpainted.

'I put this up a year or two back, just before the wife died. She wanted somewhere we could sit and look out.' He shook his head. 'Haven't got round to finishing it.'

It occurred to me it would make a perfect space for Rachel's music room once it was completed.

'How much land do you have?'

'It comes with two and a half acres. There's a small stream at the far end, and an orchard can be included if you want it.'

He left me to look around the outside on my own because his leg was playing up.

Henry looked down at his highly polished shoes and pulled a face when he saw the four fields and muddy paths behind the cottage. He pointed to an old kitchen chair by the wall. 'Think I'll sit this one out and leave you to it, James.'

At right angles, on each side of the main building, two brick-built sheds enclosed a yard perhaps ten yards square. I popped my head into them and they both appeared serviceable for tool and crop storage, as well as potential hen or pig housings. A greenhouse ran along the back of one of them. The fields, other than a vegetable plot, clearly hadn't been used for a year or two, which offered me a blank canvas, and my mind was racing with ideas by the time I wandered back to the house.

'It seems almost perfect, Mr Perkins, but I'll need to bring my wife to have a look. Will that be all right?'

'No problem at all, Mr Given. It'll be a pleasure to meet her. You know, it does me good to think of a young couple taking over the place. Even I can see the house needs a bit of love, and the land needs to be worked. Come back whenever you want.'

We talked for a few minutes about the price and his neighbours before Henry and I walked back to the car. He turned to me as he started the engine.

'Any good, James?'

'Just the job, actually. I could see us living here. I'd prefer Kenilworth because I know it, and the house does need some work, but it's a definite possibility — the nicest I've seen so far.'

As we drove back into town, I suggested he drop me at Kendrick's factory. When we'd rolled to a stop in the carpark, he touched me on the forearm before I climbed out.

'Can I ask you a question, James?'

'Of course.'

'I don't really see it, you and the countryside. Farming? You'll be bored stiff.'

'Then I'm afraid you don't know me at all, Henry.' I smiled. 'For years before I joined the police I worked in the open, first on boats, all over the world, then fruit-picking. When we moved to France last year, I earned my living on a farm and loved it. I may have been born in a city, but I'm a country boy at heart.'

Henry laughed. 'Well, each to his own, I suppose.' He waved a hand towards a long brick building with a yard down one side. 'This is it. Alec will be inside, I expect. What time will I pick you up?'

'Don't bother. I've no idea how long I'll be, so I'll walk back.'

He drove off, leaving me in front of Kendrick's factory, which was smaller than I'd imagined, though still a decent size. Twenty windows ran along two floors, and there was a three-storey block at one end with the word 'Reception' over a glass entrance. Men in brown overalls were wheeling wooden crates on sack trucks through double doors at one end of the yard, then loading them onto lorries.

Inside, a young woman behind the desk smiled, took my name and rang to tell the boss I'd arrived. A few minutes later, Kendrick bounded down the stairs. His smile and handshake were warm, and I put aside the reservations I'd held the night before.

'James, so good of you to come. Let me take you up to meet Carol Wilkins, my secretary. She'll look after you and will know where I am if I'm not in the office.'

He led the way to the top floor and a corridor with offices on one side. The structure looked temporary, though the style suggested they'd been there for some time. Each room was divided from its neighbours, and the passageway, by cream-painted half-walls, with glazed panels above. Kendrick's secretary occupied the first one and enjoyed a grand view of the fields leading down to the River Leam. The desk, which faced the door, was tidy, as were the shelves of ledgers and filing boxes on the single solid wall in the room. To one side of these, a colour-coded chart was fixed above a huge green safe. A woman in her early fifties, with glasses and a wide smile, stood when we walked in.

'This is Carol, James. Carol, this is Mr Given. He'll be round and about for a few days, so let the men know they need to answer his questions. And you find me if I'm not here.'

'Very well, Mr Kendrick. Could I ask what he'll be asking them? Just so I can tell them to be prepared.'

Kendrick chewed his bottom lip for a moment. 'Just say he's looking at how we might improve things, for us and them. So he will want to know about people's jobs, what they do in their spare time. That sort of thing.'

Carol's eyebrows rose almost imperceptibly, just enough to show her scepticism about his proposed explanation. Regardless, she made a note on her pad, then nodded. 'I'll do that right away, Mr Kendrick.'

'Thank you, Carol. Now, I'll leave him in your capable hands. I'm sure he'll want to talk to you first. Get the lay of the land, so to speak.'

The business set in train, he shook my hand again and left.

Carol Wilkins ran a tidy and efficient office. She quickly dug out a list of the men working on the project Kendrick wanted me to look at. I'd decided to start there because the men had easy access to the drawings, without needing to justify why they wanted them.

In most factories there was some kind of record of the employees' working hours, and I asked the secretary if they had such a system.

'Oh yes, Mr Given. In the morning, when they come to work, and in the evening when they leave, everyone records their time at a machine by the entrance. We also clock out at lunchtime and if we need to leave the factory for any reason. It would only be Mr Kendrick who wouldn't do it.'

'Would it be possible to see the cards for these particular men, covering, say, the last two months?'

Carol walked to the shelves, flipped through a file on the lowest one and, a couple of minutes later, passed me what I'd asked for, then turned back to her records. 'Will you want to see Mr Parkes's cards?'

'Parkes?'

'Ernest Parkes. The poor man who was killed last month.'

'Ah, yes. You'd better give them to me. Mr Kendrick mentioned him but his name had gone out of my head.'

Carol removed another small stash and passed them over. 'Please let me have them all back before you leave, Mr Given; they're the only copies we have. Now let me find you somewhere to work.'

The small office she put me in was a few doors down the corridor from hers and lacked any furnishings other than a basic table and chair. I thanked Carol and asked if she had a plan of the factory so I could find my way around. Putting off my examination of the clocking-in cards for a few minutes, I looked out of the window until she brought me the plan and a welcome cup of tea.

'I've marked where you'll find those men. Give me a shout when you're ready to go down or if you need anything else.'

In addition to two designers there were three craftsmen closely involved: a foreman and two others. I discounted the designers as a first stop, reasoning they'd have no need to steal the plans because they'd have them in their heads anyway. I also assumed there would be other people making parts for the project, but they'd only need access to details on the specific component they were producing, not the complete set of drawings. So, if anyone was sharing secrets with Kendrick's competitors, it must be one of these three.

The clocking-in cards would show who'd arrived early or gone home late, indicating who'd had the opportunity to nose around without being disturbed. I went through all the ones Carol had provided, which covered the period since the job began. Each card covered a week, with a minimum of twenty time stamps on each, so there were well over two thousand entries to check for the three men. It could have been a tedious task but I'd been told the official start, finish and lunch times, so it was quite easy to see the patterns on each card and note anything out of the ordinary.

With my notes on the men's work patterns completed, I turned to the factory plan. When unfolded it filled the table, and it took me a minute or two to work out where I was in relation to the other parts of the building. This top floor of the three-storey block, as I'd already seen, was divided into offices; below us were a meeting room, filing and storage, and, on the ground floor, the reception area, a medical room and a kitchen. In the main factory, this floor housed the machines. Above these were the draughtsmen, designers and further storage. This was clearly a bigger enterprise than it looked from the outside.

After I'd familiarised myself with the layout, marking entrances and exits on the plan, I walked along the corridor to Carol and asked if she'd phone the special project team to tell them I was on my way. I also asked to see where drawings were kept overnight. She took me down one flight of stairs to a room with filing cabinets and a long plan chest against one wall.

'Is this room locked at night, Mrs Wilkins?'

'Not that I'm aware. It's Miss, by the way. There'd be no point in locking up; people are in and out all the time, so we'd need a lot of keyholders.'

The plan chest itself was unlocked, each of the five shallow drawers accessible to anyone, as were the filing cabinets. I wasn't sure what Kendrick's military customers might say about such lax security. I opened the top drawer and saw each set of designs was labelled with a title, customer and date. Each also had a card showing the most recent borrower. Even if I didn't understand the technicalities, there was enough information for me to identify the relevant plans for any project. The filing cabinets were equally well labelled, as

"Finance", "Sales", "Correspondence", and so on, with each drawer sorted in alphabetical order.

'Could you give me ten minutes with these, Miss Wilkins? That should be enough for me to find what I need.'

The secretary said she'd come back to check I'd had no problems, then left me to it. It was easy to locate those drawings associated with Kendrick's special project, such was the quality of the system. They'd been well used, but the users and times appeared to be random, other than two names which stood out: A Kendrick and E Parkes, who had taken the drawings for about two hours each, every time a new version had been issued. I could see why the boss would want to keep his eye on developments, but why Parkes?

There was nothing else of note, and I'd finished when Miss Wilkins returned. I congratulated her on her efficiency.

'Not my doing, I'm afraid, Mr Given. Only a system I inherited. Old Mr Kendrick, the current Mr Kendrick's father, was always a stickler for the filing being right. He'd insist on precision as much in the office as in the works.'

'Have you been here long?'

She laughed. 'Forever. I started after school and worked my way up. I've been here well over thirty years and been young Mr Kendrick's secretary for about fifteen years, staying with him when his father stepped back.'

At the stairwell, Carol went up, me down, and I passed through to a space I recognised from my days at sea. The machinery may have been different on the factory floor to an engine room, but the clatter and rattle were the same, as was the smell of oil and industry. I picked my way between the lathes, grinders and milling machines, ignoring the curious glances of the operators, until I reached the team I was looking for.

Their work area lay in one corner and was separated from the rest of the factory by screens on three sides, two sets of drawings taped on one of them, and a blackboard on another, above a full-length bench with vices and what looked like a drill. Other machine tools lined the third side, and two tables the fourth. The eldest of the three men there, looking to be in his mid-forties, looked up from the table where he sat.

'You Mr Given?' he asked. I confirmed and he continued, 'Miss Wilkins said you'd be down. I'm Alfie Wilson. Foreman.' He nodded in the direction of a man my own age. 'That's Charlie Bakewell, and the young 'un's Billy Carson. How can we help you?'

Wilson didn't get up from his seat, and his sour face told me he didn't feel like helping me at all.

'I expect you've all been told I want to have a word with you, and I'll have you all upstairs in my office, one at a time, shortly. But first, tell me about the work you're doing here. In as much detail as you can to someone who's not an expert.'

The one called Carson scratched his head, grinned and challenged me in exactly the way I was expecting. 'If you're not an expert, as you've just said, what are you going to be able to tell us about the job?'

'Hmm. I always get that question, no matter where I go. The fact is, I'm an expert in my own field. Let's call it investigating. Face it, most people learn their skills from the men before them. I'd put money on Mr Wilson here passing his experience on to Charlie, and Charlie, in his turn, passing it on to you, Billy. So it's gone on for years. Now, along the way, some things change. Machines improve, materials come from different places, or the layout of the workshop changes, and so little inefficiencies creep in. Get my drift?'

'I expect so.'

'If you can explain the work you do in small enough portions, then I can spot these, because I'm not following the way you've always done it. Like a detective, I'm looking for tiny clues. Of course, if I find any, I'll run any new ideas past you men so you can agree or tell me I've got it wrong. You know the job inside out, after all.'

Carson looked at his foreman and Wilson rubbed his chin, then nodded an affirmation to the others. Finally, he stood and walked over, talked me through the workspace, the machines they were using, and the project in general terms. He explained that the customer had been contracted to supply fighter planes to the Royal Air Force and was seeking improvements to the machine gun mountings and linkages. Kendrick's had a reputation for precision in small components, so they'd been approached to come up with some ideas.

'And have you?'

The foreman shrugged. 'We're getting there. At least, the designers have. Charlie, Billy and me are just trying to make them work. Not as easy as it sounds.'

'I'm sure it doesn't sound easy at all. I've nothing but admiration for your skill. Tell me about these gun mounts.'

Wilson spent a further five minutes pointing out details on the plans and on several parts on the workbench, all of which went over my head. I nodded and asked what I hoped were intelligent questions. The smirks exchanged between Carson and Bakewell showed this hope was a vain one. I cut my losses.

'Now, who's coming upstairs to see me first?'

I spent the next three quarters of an hour talking to the three men. Billy Carson, the most junior, drew the short straw to start. I'd needed to fetch another chair from Carol's office and asked if there was any chance of a pot of tea. She'd brought it through, and Carson seemed pleased to be getting an extra break in his shift. He was in his mid- to late-twenties, tall and gangly, with a grin which looked permanent until I began my questions. I'd interviewed too many people to see this as an admission of guilt; some folks are just plain frightened of coppers. The young man had no obvious disability, so I asked why he hadn't been conscripted into the army.

'Because we're working on a military project, I'm excused. Charlie is as well. I wanted to join up, but the boss said I'd be more use here than being shot at overseas.' He blushed. 'I'm not sure if he's right or not. A lot of my friends are gone. And it's as easy to be killed here, if you think about it.'

'You mean like Ernest Parkes?'

'Yeah. Stupid accident. Ernie works all his life in this place then falls off a ladder when no-one's here to help.'

'These things happen.'

'That's what I'm saying. Hard to fathom with Ernie. Always so careful. Telling me off half the time for leaving machines on when I'm changing tools. Anyway, right or wrong, the boss thinks I'm better off here. How come you're not in the forces?'

I explained about the injured leg, missing out how it happened, and then we talked about his aspect of the project. Carson's grin returned as he explained how he produced rough components from the drawings.

'I get them within a few thousandths of an inch, then Charlie Bakewell does the finishing. He's really good. No-one better, not even old Wilson.'

I pulled his clocking-in cards from the pile on my table and fanned them out in front of him. 'You stay late most nights, Billy?'

'I do, just around half an hour.'

'Can I ask why?'

'It's the girlfriend. She works at a solicitor's office down the road and doesn't finish until six, so I stay around here then walk down to meet her.'

'And what would you do in that time?'

'Usually I'd just carry on with the job or spend a bit extra on cleaning the machines. Depends what we've been doing; sometimes it can all get a bit oily. The foreman's often here as well so I might do something for him, though he knows I don't get paid for the extra time and doesn't ask unless it's urgent.'

'Do you ever go upstairs to where the plans are kept?'

'Before I leave, do you mean?'

'Especially then, but any time really.'

'Sometimes. But what's this about? Can't see what that has to do with efficiency.'

I laughed. 'Not much, I suppose, but you never know. I only thought that if the men were up and down the stairs all day, it might make sense to move the plans to a space nearer to you.'

The cogs in Carson's head whirred for a few moments, then he nodded at my explanation. 'Might be an idea, but blokes from all over the place, upstairs and down, need to get to different drawings, so what suits us wouldn't suit them. As for going up there, I'd not be likely to take the designs back after hours, nor pick them up for next day. Mr Wilson doesn't like them lying about where they could go astray. Now and again he might hang on to them until he leaves, if there's something he's working on. Then he'd put them away himself.'

'You said he'd be here the same time as you?'

'Some nights. I expect that's how he gets to be foreman, always happy to put in the extra hours.'

I asked him a few more questions about the details of his work, and he explained he'd trained as a tool-maker so was proficient on all the machines, though his special skill was on the grinder. He puffed out his chest.

'Even better than the other two, and Charlie and old Wilson are the best engineers in the whole factory. That's why they're on this special team.'

'It's really useful to know this, Billy. You've been helpful. Can we move on for a minute? What do you do with your spare time?' I wasn't remotely interested, but Alec Kendrick had set up the charade so I had to follow it through.

'Well, as I said, there's the girlfriend. I see her most nights. We go to the pictures or for a walk. On Friday nights we might go to the pub if I've a few bob to spare. Once a month I go out with my mates on a Saturday night, and on Sunday mornings I play football.'

I made a few notes and then asked him to send one of the others up.

Charlie Bakewell looked like a man who knew his way round a factory. He wore blue overalls and heavy boots, and he was stocky and dark-haired. The nicotine yellow on his fingers shone through the ingrained oil. He'd be about my age, and stroked his moustache as he sat.

'What can I do for you, sir?'

'Have you spoken to Billy, Mr Bakewell?'

'Only in passing. He came down, said you'd a bunch of questions and wanted to talk to me next.'

We went through the same ones I'd asked his workmate and he confirmed what Carson had told me about his work.

'He's a good lad, Billy. Conscientious and methodical. Has this daft manner about him but he knows how to work a machine and doesn't need telling twice what's expected. Magician on the grinder too. Just not had as much experience as me on the others, so I get to do the more precise adjustments before Alfie ... Mr Wilson ... checks they all fit together.'

'You seem to stay late on Wednesdays. Why is that?'

'Some of the lads go for a drink that night. We were apprentices here, and once a week we meet a couple of old mates who now work at other factories nearby. The Crown doesn't open until seven so we go and have our tea at a café in town, then go on to the pub. Is this important?'

'No. Just trying to get a picture. I believe Miss Wilkins has explained we're looking at improving work and the social side of your lives. If some of you played football, for example, like Billy Carson does, Mr Kendrick might consider making a donation to the club so you'd have better facilities. Make sense?'

'I suppose so,' Bakewell grinned. 'Wouldn't be putting a few pints behind the bar, though, would he?'

'Tell me about your foreman.'

Bakewell shook his head. 'I'm not snitching on no-one. Alfie's decent.'

'I'm not asking you to snitch, Charlie, unless there's something to snitch about? Is there?'

'No.'

'Then your description of him as "decent" is the sort of thing I want to know. I'm not trying to trick you. You get on with him?'

'As I said, he's a good bloke. Works all the hours there are and looks after a sick wife. I'll not say anything bad about him. I've had worse foremen as well.'

'Then that's all I need for now. You can go. Send him up when you get back, will you?'

It took another ten minutes before Wilson appeared, during which time I looked out of the window at the river gliding through the fields. A family of ducks rested on the far bank, and a moorhen scooted into the shelter of a weeping willow, startled by a passer-by. Wilson knocked on the door and I called him in.

He'd removed the brown warehouse coat he'd had on downstairs in favour of a herringbone jacket, which I imagined he wore when meeting his boss. He was civil but answered my questions with the minimum of elaboration. He may have been a man of few words, or he might have been avoiding giving anything away, but I had to probe to get him to go much further than one-word answers. After the first few attempts at conversation, I knew I needed to tackle him.

'Listen, Mr Wilson, you seem reticent to answer my questions. Why?'

'I don't know what you're talking about. I've not refused to answer, have I?'

'Not quite, but you're not helping. You do understand Mr Kendrick, your employer, has asked me to carry out this exercise?'

'I do, and if he'd asked me beforehand I'd have told him it's a waste of time. It's more, and better, engineers we need, not men like you trying to get us to work harder for the same money.'

'Then perhaps you need to take that up with him when we're finished — unless you want us to go to see him now?'

'What would be the point? He's taken you on and he isn't going to change his decision on my account, is he? No, you'd best get on with it.' He leaned back in his chair. 'I'm sorry, Mr Given, I know it's not your fault. It's just that with everything else going on, the last thing I need is for the boss to be chasing his profits. Ask away, and I'll do my best to tell you what you need.'

I could see Wilson's point. Factory workers, even ones as valuable as him, didn't always get the best deal from their employers when customers were hard to find, like in wartime. I pressed on with the interview and showed him his clocking-in cards.

'You're in work well after your time every night, Mr Wilson. Is there a reason for this?'

Wilson snorted. 'Huh. Shows you know nothing about a factory.'

'Tell me.'

'Always something to do. Every customer wants his stuff last week.'

'But you're not going to get it done working an extra hour, are you?'

'No. Didn't say I would. But I can make sure everything done that day is right, and we're all ready for the next one.'

'And that's what you do?'

'Said so, didn't I?'

I stood, walked across to the window and leant my back against it. 'I'm told you sometimes hang on to copies of the designs when the other men have gone. Is that right?'

'If I have to. Why?'

'Just asking. Is there a particular reason?'

Wilson shrugged. 'No.'

'Do you ever take them home?'

'No. Never.'

'That's fine. Can I ask you about your spare time?'

'Spare time?'

'Yes, what do you do outside work.'

'Like most married men of my age, I expect, I go home, have my dinner and listen to the wireless with my wife. Sunday lunchtime I might take a walk to the pub, if I've a few bob to spare, which isn't often. That's about it. Listen, is there much more of this? I've a job to do, and it isn't getting done with me on my backside answering your daft questions.'

'No, not just now. You can go. I'll let you know when I've done my report for Mr Kendrick, and I'll have you in again to go through it, to make sure it makes at least some sense.'

When he left, still muttering under his breath, I scribbled a few notes but I was no wiser than when I'd started. All three men stayed later than their required hours, two of them frequently but, in itself, it meant nothing. Only Wilson appeared reluctant to talk freely, but that could just have been his annoyance at the pressure he was under from his boss.

A few minutes later, the klaxon sounded to mark the end of the working day. I waited another half hour then retraced my steps downstairs to the machine shop door. Through the glass I could see most of the room was in darkness, the only area still lit being where the special team worked. Bakewell appeared to have left and Carson had his jacket on, ready to go. I was in half a mind to follow him, but watched the foreman for a little while instead. I assumed the younger man wouldn't chance taking drawings away with Wilson still there, so I'd need to go after him another night if this one proved fruitless.

Alfie Wilson had his head down at his table, examining something I couldn't see. He consulted his watch several times. After a quarter of an hour, he stood and looked around the room, causing me to duck out of sight. When I looked back, he had his coat on and was rooting in the bottom of a cupboard. I left through the reception door, staying hidden as best I could, and watched for Wilson leaving at the other end of the yard.

I didn't have to wait long. When he emerged, he was carrying a brown leather briefcase.

I telephoned Kendrick as soon as I arrived back at Henry Dyer's house.

'I think I've found your man.'

'Thank God. Who is it, James?'

'I'd rather not say until I'm sure. I've got to go back to Birmingham, so I won't be able to deal with it until next weekend. I'll need to chat to the men again, but I'll let you know the outcome straight after I have.'

'So you think it's one of them?'

'Well, it seems to me they're the only ones with the opportunity and enough knowledge to know what they'd be taking. But leave it until I've had that talk and we should know for certain.'

Kendrick pressed me for more information and I refused again, so he agreed to wait, then hung up.

It was far too late to think about going back to Birmingham. My thigh was burning with pain, and I knew the walk from the station to home would be beyond me. Henry insisted I stayed for another night, so I begged a couple of aspirin and excused myself for a lie down while Audrey prepared a meal.

When I got down to the table, Henry was finishing a sherry. He poured another large one straight away. His flushed cheeks suggested they'd not been the first of the night.

We began to share anecdotes we'd missed the previous night about our ex-colleagues in the force. A boss is always a boss, rarely a friend, even when you've both moved on, and our years working together was all we had in common. Returning to this line of conversation was inevitable. Henry had little respect for the officers above and around him, accusing them of being pen-pushers and bureaucrats, keener on office politics than solving crimes. The more he emptied his glass, the more he spoke through gritted teeth. It was clear his last years in the police hadn't been happy. I was beginning to regret having agreed to spend the extra night when Audrey brought through mutton chops, potatoes and cabbage. I complimented her and she said the chops were the last the butcher had. Henry wanted every detail of what I'd been doing, and I had to be careful to avoid Wilson's name because I was sure it would be passed on to Kendrick the next morning.

After dinner my hosts insisted we had a few hands of cards so we played rummy, a game which I'd always disliked but it suited an odd number of players and, to my mind, demanded little concentration. For me, the challenge wasn't there, and if rummy was the game I'd been introduced to when I was young, I doubted the cards would have become such an obsession. I won most hands and we passed a pleasant hour chatting, with Henry now working his way down a bottle of brandy. As the light faded, Henry switched on the wireless for the news and I followed Audrey into the kitchen to help with the washing up.

We'd almost finished and I was drying the last pan, when Audrey dropped her voice to a whisper.

'Can I tell you something, James?'

'Of course, what is it?'

'It's about —' She swung her head towards the door as Henry pushed it open.

He chuckled. 'Just came for another drink. Nothing but doom and gloom on the wireless. Thought I'd have a nightcap, then off to bed.' He put an arm round his wife's shoulder. 'What do you say, old girl?'

Audrey lifted his hand away. 'You go up, dear. I'll follow in a minute.'

Henry grinned again and swayed to the living room. I heard him stumble on the stairs, so well out of earshot. I asked Audrey what it was she'd been about to say.

'Oh, it's nothing, James. We'll perhaps talk about it another time. I'd best join Henry. He'll only be down again if I'm not there in the next few minutes.'

After I'd helped put away the final dishes, Audrey checked that all the doors and windows were locked. She did this twice, then returned and checked the kitchen door again before turning off the light.

It took me an age to drop off to sleep, partly due to the meal lying heavy in my stomach, but also because I was wondering why Audrey was so security-conscious. What had she wanted to tell me? Clearly something about Henry, because she'd shut up the minute he'd disturbed us. It wouldn't be anything to do with Kendrick's problems, though I couldn't figure out what else it might be. In the end, I decided she may have wanted to talk about her husband's drinking, which seemed to have become an issue not in evidence when he'd been at work. I'd been to plenty of events over the years, and he'd always stuck to a respectable number of drinks. Perhaps his retirement was having a bigger impact than he was letting on.

Next morning the dawn chorus woke me at first light and I spent a couple of hours drifting in and out of sleep until I couldn't face lying in bed a minute longer. I tiptoed along the landing, washed and shaved, then returned and dressed. For another half an hour I sat on the chair in the window bay and watched pigeons pecking around on the bowling green opposite. Eventually I wandered downstairs, but I hadn't a clue where to find the materials to make a cup of tea so I sat in the kitchen, taking in the garden. At this time of the morning, with much of it still in shade, the colours were muted and dew covered the lawn. The coolness appealed and I went to open the back door. I noticed a recently re-glazed pane, the putty as yet unpainted, as I reached for the handle. Before I could step outside, Audrey walked into the kitchen and, once her startled look disappeared, she smiled.

'You should have tapped the door, James. I've only been reading in bed. Shall I make tea?'

'Please.'

With the ease developed from much practice, she moved round the kitchen, lifting plates from the dresser, lighting the gas under the kettle, and putting bread under the grill. All this was accompanied by her commenting on the fine weather and telling me how much Henry was enjoying his retirement, giving the lie to my thoughts of the previous night. In no time there were a pot, two cups, toast, butter and marmalade on the table, and Audrey took a seat opposite me.

'There now. Tuck in.'

'Won't we wait for Henry?'

She gave a tinkling laugh. 'No, I don't think so. He'll be at least another hour. As I said, he's taking his retirement seriously. He's never up much before nine, or even nine-thirty. He'll get out of bed in about thirty minutes, take a long bath, then shave and dress. Later, he'll almost certainly be on the golf course if this sunshine hangs around.'

'I thought the course was closed.'

'Oh, it is, but that doesn't stop Henry walking all eighteen holes whenever he can. Sometimes he'll make the pretence of taking a single club and ball with him, but I know it's just for the exercise.' Audrey winked. 'At least it gets him out of my hair for a while.'

'Does he go up there every day, then?'

'Usually only at weekends. Sometimes during the week he might go up in the evening, finishing with a pint or two at the nineteenth hole. Monday to Friday he stays closer to home for his walk, through the park, along the river then back round.'

We both tucked into breakfast. After my third cup of tea, I said I should be leaving for my train.

'Before I go, though, can I ask what you were going to tell me last night? If you don't want Henry to know, I promise I'll keep it to myself.'

Audrey glanced away and bit her bottom lip. 'It's possibly just me being silly, but I'm worried about him.'

'Is he ill?'

'No, nothing like that. There have been a few odd things happening recently, and his mind seems to be elsewhere some days.'

'What kind of things?'

'Well, as Henry said last night, we think our dog, Ben, was poisoned. Before then, we had a broken window.' She pointed at the back door. 'That one.'

'You were burgled?'

'No, that's what's strange. Whoever did it could easily have put their hand through, opened the door and come inside but, as far as we could tell, they didn't bother. Nothing was missing, and even though it had been raining there were no signs of footsteps on the floor.'

'Maybe they were disturbed before they could get inside.'

'Perhaps.' Audrey folded her arms and glanced out into the garden for a few moments. 'Then, the same week, Henry left the car on the drive for an hour and went out to find two flat tyres. When the garage looked at them, they weren't punctured. Let down on purpose, they said.'

'Apart from the dog, it sounds like a youngster playing tricks. Has Henry upset someone? Kept a lad's football or something?'

Audrey said they'd discussed the possibilities without coming up with anything. 'I do hope it is just some nipper with nothing better to do, but you never know, do you? Henry was in the police force a long time.'

'I can't see it's that. Henry was at a desk for the back end of his career and hadn't arrested anyone in many a year. If it was some villain bearing a serious grudge, they'd have held it for a long time, and I'm sure they'd then do more than break a window and let down his tyres. Admittedly, attempting to kill your dog takes it up a notch, but it could be that they're not connected. You said Henry had something on his mind. Perhaps this is what he's been thinking about. Are you sure you don't want me to have a word with him?'

'It's probably better if you don't. If he thinks I'm concerned, then he'll fret even more. As I said, it's probably something and nothing.'

'Well, let me know if anything else out of the ordinary occurs, and we'll see what we can find out.'

Audrey leant across the table and squeezed the back of my hand. 'Thank you, James. It's a comfort to know I can call on you.'

I helped wash the dishes, retrieved Saturday night's Birmingham newspaper from the sitting room, and ten minutes later I was hurrying to the station, looking forward to getting back to Rachel.

FIVE

Thursday 4th July, 1940

My week went much as the previous one, ticking off the hours in my father's workshop and spending evenings scouring the newspapers for houses we might like. There were plenty of places advertised in the city, and some bigger farms out in the country, but nothing which would suit us.

On Thursday, over our evening meal, Rachel and I talked about our hunt and agreed we might need to abandon the idea or widen our horizons. I suggested I telephone the best of the ones we'd already viewed to see if there'd been any change.

'Well, I loved the one in Kenilworth. You could see if Mrs Harris has spoken to her farmer neighbour about more land.'

'I liked it as well, but you didn't see Perkins's place near Leamington. You'd have snapped it up, Rachel. We'll need to go over and you can take a look.'

'I thought you preferred Kenilworth?'

'I do, but that's just me being a stick-in-the-mud. I lived and worked there for such a long time. Leamington is a fine town, and the farm is perfect. Admittedly, the house needs a bit of work, but that means we can get it just how we'd like it, and for a decent price.'

Rachel stood and began clearing the table. 'You know I'm still not convinced about this move, don't you, James?'

'Yes. But you did say you'd consider it.'

'And I am. But I'm not prepared to take a house that's second-best just because it's some idea you have in your head about your ideal life.'

Before I could reply, the telephone rang. I hadn't expected to hear from Henry Dyer again for a while, so I was surprised to hear his voice when I answered.

'James? I'm sorry to disturb you at this time of the evening. Can you talk?'

'Of course. We've eaten and I was just about to help with the dishes. Is there something wrong? More problems at Kendrick's?'

'No, no, nothing like that. Well, not exactly. Alec is happy with the way things are going. Says you should consider a new career as a private detective. Thinks you'd get a constant stream of customers with his recommendation. Wealthy divorcees wanting their new suitors checked out, husbands convinced their wives are deceiving them. Easy money, I'd say.'

'Not sure it's for me, Henry. I always preferred proper villains to confidence tricksters and cheats. That's not why you've rung though, is it?' The line went quiet for a moment. 'Henry?'

'Sorry. No, it isn't. I've not had a good day and wanted to hear a friendly voice. My mother passed away this morning.'

Now it was my turn to gather my thoughts. 'That's awful, Henry, you must be upset.'

'Well, I am and I'm not. She wasn't a young woman, and not in the best of health these past few years, so it's a blessing in some ways. But we were close, and I'm sad to lose her. Although you didn't know her, I'm sure you'd have got on; she had a wonderful sense of humour and an enquiring mind.'

'Still, it's never easy when someone you love dies. Is there anything I can do?'

'It's kind of you to offer, James, but I just wanted to let you know and to ask you to leave Alec's case for a couple of weeks until Mum's funeral is out of the way. I've spoken to him and he's fine about it in the circumstances.'

'Would you like me to come to the funeral?'

'There's no need. Audrey is rock-solid and she'll be by my side. Funny what goes through your head at times like these. All day I've had a song in my head, one Mum and Dad danced to whenever they were out. They met soon after she left service, you know, and both loved to dance. Mum had been a maid to a rich family, and Dad had been an army doctor out in South Africa and was just setting up his practice here in Leamington.'

'Is your father still alive?'

'No, he went about thirty years ago, so Mum and I became very close.'

I let him reminisce about his mother for a while longer until he petered out. I asked if he was all right.

'Mustn't get maudlin, James. She lived to a good age and had a fine life. As I said, I'll miss her, but we have to go on. I'll call you after her funeral and you must come to stay again. Finish that job you've started.'

I told him I'd enjoy another visit, and, hopefully, convince Rachel to join me the next time.

SIX

Audrey Dyer's telephone call came ten minutes after we'd cleared the dishes from our evening meal.

'James. You've got to come. Henry has disappeared.'

'Disappeared how?'

'He ... he went for a walk —' great sobs punctuated her words — 'this morning ... with the dog ... and he's not come back.'

'You had an argument?'

'No, not at all. Something's happened to him. I know it has. You must come, I don't know who else to turn to.'

'Have you been to the police?'

'I went in this afternoon after I'd looked for him. They said it was too early to do anything and I should leave it a day or two.'

'Perhaps they're right. Maybe he's just decided to take some time away.'

'Henry would never do such a thing without telling me, and why would he abandon the dog? He's not taken a change of clothes or anything.'

'What's this about the dog?'

Audrey explained Henry had been up at around nine o'clock as usual. He'd eaten his breakfast and pottered in the garden, leaving the house to walk the dog just after eleven. He'd said he'd be going over the river then along the other bank and back through the park. This walk normally lasted about three quarters of an hour, maybe a little longer if he took a club and golf ball for some practice. He hadn't that morning. She'd become concerned when he didn't arrive home for lunch by one, but didn't go to look for him for another hour in case he'd wandered into town, as he sometimes did. When she went to find him, Audrey had followed the route Henry had said he was taking, and she'd found their Jack Russell wandering home.

'The dog even had his lead on, so he hadn't simply run away when released for a run about. Ben never does, anyway. He always stays close.'

'And you're sure nothing happened between you to make Henry want to spend a day out?'

'There wasn't anything, James. He was in a good mood when he left. Can you come over and help? Please.'

'I'm sorry, Audrey. I can't just drop everything here in Birmingham and come to Leamington, and I think the police are right. Leave it a day or two. If I start poking around over there, it won't go down well when the police decide to investigate. Let's leave it until tomorrow evening, and if you've not heard from Henry by then we'll decide what to do. Is that all right?'

Audrey wasn't happy, and pressed me further, but I stuck to my guns.

Rachel came through from the kitchen as I hung up. 'Who was that?'

I told her what Audrey had said. She pondered for a moment, then shook her head.

'You're not going to become involved, are you, James?'

'I don't think so.'

Rachel went to her music room to prepare some lessons. Henry occupied my thoughts all evening, and I couldn't settle to the wireless. Instead, I tried to take my mind off Audrey's telephone call by digging out a pack of cards and playing solitaire, but I gave it up after half an hour. I picked up the newspaper and flung it aside ten minutes later, my concentration too shot to bother. In the end, I pulled my notepad from our sideboard drawer, and began recording what Audrey had told me.

SEVEN

Tuesday 16th July, 1940

The night was hot and humid, and I tossed and turned through the small hours, my head full of Audrey's call. When I nodded off, nightmares about broken bodies and past cases woke me over and over, until my alarm broke through. When I took Rachel her cup of tea, I started our usual morning chat.

'How did you sleep?'

'Well. You?'

'Terrible. Hardly a wink.'

'This is because of that call, James..'

'It was just the weather. Too sticky.'

'The weather be damned. It was just the same for me and I was out like a baby. I could tell when we came to bed, you'd been thinking about Henry all evening.' Her cup rattled as she lifted it from its saucer. 'But let's be clear. I won't have you putting yourself in danger again.'

'What danger? All we know is Henry didn't arrive home after his morning walk and his wife, quite reasonably, is worried.'

'You're not a fool, James, and neither am I, so don't treat me like one. Henry wouldn't just go off like that without good reason. You think something's happened to him, don't you?'

I hung my head. 'Yes, I do.'

'Then use your police contacts and get them to investigate. Don't you dare try to do it yourself. Last time you got caught up in that kind of thing, you could have been killed.' She put her hand in mine. 'I couldn't bear to lose you.'

During my last three investigations, I'd been almost shot and poisoned. I had also been stabbed, as well as tortured and beaten, so Rachel's concerns weren't without foundation. We sat for a while, quietly holding hands, until I had to leave.

'Look, I have to go or else Papa will blow a fuse. I've told Audrey she should leave it to the police, so I'll speak to her when I get home and see if Henry's turned up. If he hasn't, and the police still won't intervene, we can talk about what I'm to do. You know I can't just leave it there.'

Rachel moved her hand away. 'I know, but go now and we'll talk this evening.'

I went downstairs, drew back the blackout curtains in the living room, lifted my lunch from the kitchen table, and left the house on to quiet streets. Rachel's house was in a part of Birmingham where most people didn't go to work early. They managed offices or ran small businesses. They were the sort of people whose children attended the better schools and who, in the days before the last war, would have had at least one live-in maid. As a consequence, the gardens were well tended, and the curtains still drawn when I made my way through the airless morning. It was only when I neared Great Hampton Street that I saw much life, where labourers and shop workers were leaving their houses, and lorries, buses and cars droned down the main road towards the city centre. Crossing the street, I joined others like myself, heading for jobbing workshops where, for many, the days were long and the pay barely adequate. These men and women kept the country running while so many had been called up to join the forces. Many of the young men walked with fear in their eyes, expecting every day to bring a letter from the War Office requesting the pleasure of their company. I knew I was one of the lucky ones, exempt from service because of injury, and enjoying the privilege of my father's goodwill.

All morning I kept my mind occupied by immersing myself in paperwork — writing to suppliers, paying bills and bringing the accounts up to date, as I tended to do on Tuesdays. I checked the order book, walked to the bank to deposit some cheques, and even tidied my desk. Anything which stopped me dwelling on what may have happened to Henry.

I almost telephoned Audrey to ask if she'd had any news, but spotted my father on the prowl so kept my nose to the grindstone. At lunchtime I sat with him and went through the figures I'd produced earlier. He smiled at the bottom line but not at me. After I'd eaten my sandwiches, I nipped upstairs to say hello to Mama. In her excitable and meandering way, she took a full fifteen minutes to tell me all that had happened at the weekend, which was nothing much. By the time she'd finished, I had to go back down to drag through the afternoon.

The Dyers' phone rang for a long time, and I was about to hang up when Audrey answered. She sounded like she had the weight of the world on her shoulders.

'Oh, James, it's you. I'd nodded off in the chair. Not much sleep last night, and I'd been out all day wandering the town looking for Henry.'

'He's not back, then?'

'No.' There was a long pause. 'Nobody's seen him. I went round the park, and to the watering holes he uses, but he's not been in. Nor has he been in any of his favourite shops. I even walked to the golf course with the dog, hoping Henry might have changed his mind about where he'd walk and Ben would lead me to him, but no luck. At one point, Ben dragged me into a clump of trees, barking his head off, but it was only a rabbit. I asked three or four men who were walking the course if they'd seen Henry. They all knew him, but none had seen him in the last few days.'

'Any word from the police?'

'I called in this afternoon. Their answer was just the same. Give it another couple of days, they said. You wouldn't think he'd been their boss for so long, would you? Treated just like anyone else.'

'Would it help if I had a word?'

'What would help, James, is if you jumped on the train and came over here. You, of all people, owe it to him.'

'That's not fair, Audrey, and you know it. I've no authority to investigate. The police have. Regardless of what Henry means to me, it's them you need to convince to act, not some ex-policeman who you think owes you a favour.'

'But you could at least come to Leamington and have a word with them. You must still have some influence.'

I didn't want to argue with Audrey, knowing what she must be going through. I told her to give me the night to think about what we might do next, then I put down the receiver, wondering how I could convince Rachel of the only way I could see forward. I assumed she wouldn't stand in my way, but she wasn't going to make it easy either. My wife had made her position plain: she didn't want me playing at being a policeman anymore.

Rachel folded her arms and raised an eyebrow when I hung up. 'Well?'

'Audrey wants me to go over.'

'So will you?'

'I don't want to, for lots of reasons, but Audrey's right, Rachel. I do owe Henry this much. I think he suspected for a long time that I was Jewish, but it didn't matter to him. Others

74

in the force would have despised me for it, but not Henry. Plenty did after it came out. As long as I did my job and got results, Henry would stand up for me.'

Rachel shrugged. 'You're going to do it, then? I can see I can't stop you.'

I didn't answer for a moment, trying to think of an alternative. Nothing came. 'I'll go over tomorrow. See if I can find anything. Talk to the local man. If I can convince him to pick it up, I'll be home for teatime.'

'And if not?'

I took a deep breath. 'Then I may have to stay for a day or two.'

Even as I said it, I knew Rachel's objection wasn't the only hurdle I'd need to overcome.

NINE

Wednesday 17th July, 1940

As I'd expected, my father wasn't happy with my request. As always, I played the peacemaker in our relationship, and took a cup of tea to his workbench, where he sat on his high stool. He looked up, laid down his scissors and pushed away the garment he'd been working on. He nodded at the drink.

'To what do I owe this, Jacob? You must want something.'

'I need to take the rest of the day off.'

'What?'

'I think you heard me, Papa. Henry Dyer, my old superintendent, has gone missing. His wife's asked me to look for him.'

'But, Jacob, you can't keep doing this. Either you're working for me or you're not.'

'Papa, when I came back from France, you knew I wouldn't be here for long. Just until I found my feet again. All the paperwork is up to date, and there's not really anything else for me to do. Don't get me wrong, I'm grateful for the job, but you know it's not what I want. Not what I've ever wanted.'

He'd never understood why I had no desire to follow him into tailoring. His insistence had forced me away from home when I was sixteen. A fondness for cutting and sewing cloth hadn't blossomed in the two decades since.

'If a friend of yours had vanished, you'd want to help his wife find him, wouldn't you?'

'Of course.'

'And when I was still employed by the police, you never questioned me taking time off to look for your brother in France, did you?'

'That was different. Flesh and blood. We'd lost touch, and I thought he might need help.'

'Then that's all I'm trying to do. Henry left home a couple of days ago, supposedly taking his dog for a walk, and he hasn't come back. His poor wife is distraught, the police aren't interested and she's asked for my assistance. Do you want me to say no?'

He was in a corner, and my father didn't like being in a corner. He lifted his scissors and slammed them back down on his bench, rattling the cup in its saucer. 'Do what you want, Jacob. You always do. Go off if you need to, but we'll need a long, hard talk when you come back. And you'll take the time as unpaid holiday.'

I apologised again, and told him I hoped to only be away for the day, but he'd stopped listening, focusing all his attention on the army officer's uniform in front of him. I went back to my desk, telephoned Audrey, told her I'd be over in an hour, and grabbed my coat.

The morning had been dry and humid when I'd walked to work, but a storm erupted as I left and drenched me on my way to the station, making me wish I'd invested in a taxi. The platforms glistened in the rain and the air felt thick. Thunder rumbled and tumbled under the canopy. The shower dragged the temperature down, and I was grateful when the Leamington train arrived and I was able to climb on board.

Even though the rain had been heavy, it passed quickly and the Leamington streets were already dry by the time I arrived, though the forecast said there'd be showers all day. My damp clothes felt increasingly clammy as I wandered through the late morning sunshine to the Dyer's house.

Audrey met me at the door, a long way from the well turned-out woman I'd met on my previous visits. She had no hint of make-up, and her slippers and slightly creased dress emphasised her pale cheeks and worried expression. She looked on the edge of tears.

'Thank the Lord you've come, James. There's still no word.'

Inside, I asked her to explain again what had happened the morning Henry left.

'There was nothing unusual, really. Henry got up and had breakfast as normal. Although he was in a good mood, his mind seemed elsewhere. I asked him about it, but he laughed and said it was just something he'd been trying to puzzle out. I wasn't sure I believed him, but he insisted there was nothing wrong. He took Ben's lead and the two of them set off, leaving me with the dishes and my Ladies' Circle paperwork to get on with.' A tear escaped and ran down her cheek. 'That was the last time I saw him.'

'You said "nothing unusual" happened. But there was something, wasn't there?'

'Only another of these odd incidents we'd been getting. I told you about the dog being poisoned, the broken window and the flat tyres. Well, when I got up on Monday morning I found washing all around the garden. I'd forgotten to take it off the line the night before. I thought it must have been windy and it had blown down, but Henry said there'd been no wind. He checked the side gate and it was wide open, even though Henry was sure he'd bolted it before locking the house for the night at suppertime. Something else he is always careful about. He always says I'm too trusting.'

'Another prank, then?'

'What else could it be? There has been lots of small stuff as well, though nothing serious. Plants lifted from the border, mud smeared on the front step, those kind of things. If Henry wasn't so meticulous about his garden and the outside of the house, we probably wouldn't even have noticed some of them. I have to say, though, the thing with the washing scared me. I asked him to have a word at the police station.'

'Did he?'

'I don't think so. He wouldn't have had a chance. They didn't mention it when I went in, anyway.'

'Has anything happened since Henry disappeared?'

Audrey thought for a moment, her head on one side. 'Not that I've noticed, though my mind has been elsewhere, as you'd expect. You think they're connected, then?'

'Not necessarily, but possibly. You're sure you can't think of anyone who might have a grudge?'

'No-one.' Hailstones suddenly rattled on the kitchen window. 'What do you think we should do?'

'I'll call round to the police station, see if I can have a word, then I'll retrace Henry's usual steps if you give me directions.'

'Well, you can't go out in this weather. I'll make us tea while it blows through.'

Audrey explained how Henry was a creature of habit. He had his regular walks, cafés he went to, favourite pubs, golf on certain days, and wireless programmes he preferred.

'That's why I'm so worried, James. It's so unlike him to do anything out of the ordinary. We'll have been married for forty years in a fortnight, and you get to know a man in that time.' Her shoulders shook as the tears began to flood down her cheeks. 'Something awful has happened to him, I'm certain it has.'

Inspector Bob Moore leant back in his chair and rubbed his cheeks. He was a thin man in his late fifties, and he was barely minimum regulation height. I suspected he'd been drafted back into the force at Inspector level to fill a gap left by younger men leaving for the army. We'd met from time to time at meetings when I'd just been promoted, and he'd always struck me as solid — as solid as the station he was housed in, a two-storey square block with impressive steps and a columned entrance. Though there were men outside stacking sandbags against its walls, I thought it unlikely that Hitler's bombs would find their way to this leafy corner of Warwickshire. Moore's office was on the first floor at the back, at the same level as the railway line, and it shook each time a train rumbled past his window. Other than the inconvenience of having to pause our conversation each time a train came, his office was better than the ones I'd enjoyed in Kenilworth — particularly in my last months, when I'd been in a cellar with no windows. Moore's was spacious, with a smart fireplace for winter, and even a boldly patterned carpet. His desk was as wide as those I'd seen higher ranks sitting behind.

I told him Audrey Dyer had asked me to have a word about Henry going missing.

'I'm sorry, Mr Given. We're pretty stretched and unless we're sure a crime's been committed, I can't release anyone to look into it. I told Mrs Dyer the same thing.'

'But isn't the disappearance of a former police superintendent cause for concern? You knew him, Inspector. He'd not be one for simply going off on a whim, would he?'

'Who's to say? Recently retired, comfortably off? Time on his hands and under his wife's feet? Wouldn't be the first time.' Moore raised an eyebrow as if he knew something.

'What have you heard?'

'Listen, I'm not saying anything is going on, but I did ask some of the beat coppers if they'd seen Dyer. Only because he'd been the boss — I wouldn't have done it for anyone else.'

'And?'

'And one had seen him in a café at the weekend, looking mighty pleased with himself. Sitting with a good-looking woman a few years younger than his lady wife.'

Moore's revelation knocked me for six. I'd known Henry Dyer for years, and he'd never once struck me as the type to cheat on his wife. Still, it was only a thought, and the policeman said he didn't necessarily give it credence, only that it would prevent him starting to poke around without more evidence.

'So what kind of thing would you need, Inspector?'

'Hard to say. You know we'd normally not look at a missing person, particularly an adult, until they've been gone a while. Death threats? A body — God help me.'

'You'd have no objection to me poking around, then?'

'None at all, if you've the time and the inclination. Just don't pretend you're doing it for me.'

I left the police station and walked towards the centre of town, past shops and rooming houses, before turning down a side street to find my way to the tea shop the inspector had mentioned, a fairly dull little place with cream walls and brown tables. Not the sort of place I imagined Audrey would choose, so perhaps that was why Henry went there, as an escape where he'd not be interrupted by his wife. Most of the dozen or so tables were occupied, mainly by men tucking into substantial plates of meat and two vegetables, with the odd pair of women enjoying scones and tea. A wireless on a shelf behind the counter was playing a dance band when I took a seat and skimmed the menu. The lone waitress acknowledged me with a nod and a mouthed, 'One minute, sir,' as she delivered a tray to a group of workmen. She was as good as her word and came directly to take my order with a broad smile.

'What can I get you today, sir?'

'I'll take a pot of tea and a fruit scone if you have one left.'

She disappeared through to the kitchen while I stared out at the traffic. It had started to rain heavily since I'd arrived, and I cursed because I wasn't dressed for this weather. Lightning flashed, making the customers jump, and seconds later, thunder rattled the windows.

The waitress returned and laid down the teapot, a blue-patterned plate bearing one of the biggest scones I'd ever seen, and a jam pot. A minute later she brought me a cup and saucer matching the plate. 'Will there be anything else, sir?'

'I wonder if you can help me, Miss…'

'Ann will do, sir.'

'Then, Ann, would you know a friend of mine, a Mr Henry Dyer?'

'I do. Retired gentleman. Used to be a policeman, I believe.'

'That's right, he was. Does he come in here often?'

'Once or twice a week, sir. Usually has the same as you. Sits and reads his newspaper. Has a little dog with him. Come to think of it, he's not been in this week.'

'When was he last in?'

Ann rubbed her chin, then raised a finger in the air. 'Saturday. That's it. I remember because he paid with a ten-shilling note, and I had to hunt around for change because we bank most of it on a Friday.'

'Was he on his own?'

Ann stepped back and folded her arms. 'I'm sorry, sir, I think I've said enough. I really shouldn't be gossiping about customers.'

'No, you're right, of course, and in normal circumstances I wouldn't be asking. It's just that Henry is a friend of mine and he's not been seen since Monday, so I'm trying to trace him. His wife is beside herself.'

'Oh dear. In that case, I suppose it's all right to tell you. He was with a lady, that's why his bill was a bit more than usual. I heard him call her Doris. She's been in before, but not often. I was standing over at the counter and I saw him give her some money. Notes.' She shouted across to the workmen. 'You blokes saw Mr Dyer on Saturday, didn't you? Do you know the woman he was with?'

One of the men called back, 'Doris Wenlock. Lives in one of those houses down on Rosefield Street with her mum. Nice lady. Pretty and a good cook too, I hear. Not married, though, so there must be a problem somewhere.'

The three men laughed and got on with their lunch.

I asked Ann where Rosefield Street was, and she gave me directions. I thanked her and dived into my tea and scone, watching the rain gradually subside. As I picked away at the last few crumbs with my fingertips, I spotted someone I recognised crossing the street. A man I hadn't seen in more than a year, and never expected to see in Leamington.

Ex-Inspector Terry Gleeson was much thinner than when we'd last met at his hospital bed, but as he glanced in the café window, I'd have known his face and piggy eyes anywhere.

TEN

Wednesday 17th July, 1940

Terry Gleeson wasn't difficult to follow. I knew him well, and he'd have no idea I was in the town. Even if he had, I'd lost a good few pounds, gained a deep tan in France and let my hair grow a little longer, so he wouldn't have recognised me. He sauntered along one side of the street, then crossed back and forth to look in shop windows. I'd worked alongside him in Kenilworth, and he was bent, bigoted and vindictive. When I'd seen him in hospital, he'd been facing forced retirement and possible arrest. We hadn't parted on good terms.

After ten minutes, the shops petered out. Gleeson glanced at his watch and began to walk faster, turning into a side street. When I did the same, keeping my distance, I watched him stop outside a building, part way along the terrace. I gave him time to go inside, then walked past on the opposite pavement. The dilapidated signage across the whole length of the front read "Argyll Family and Commercial Hotel" and, on a small board on the door, it announced they had vacancies. It looked like it had been an establishment of some substance at one time, though the peeling paintwork and unwashed windows said those days had long gone. A public bar occupied the ground floor, with an entrance in the centre and a door on one side, which Gleeson had gone through. He'd used a key pulled from his pocket.

When I'd worked with him, Gleeson had lived in a nice house in Coventry, only a ten-minute walk from the city centre. He clearly hadn't served a long prison sentence for his crimes since I'd last seen him — which he should have — there hadn't been enough time. Why, then, was he now staying in a rundown commercial hotel in Leamington? His use of a key suggested he wasn't just a visitor. I hung around on the corner for quarter of an hour to see if he came out again. He didn't, so I doubled back down a parallel street and found my way to the area of town where they'd said Doris Wenlock lived.

Rosefield Street had tidy front gardens, and looked like the sort of place where everyone knew their neighbours. I only needed to ask at a couple of doors before someone pointed out the one I was looking for.

A short, slim woman, probably in her early forties, answered when I knocked. The smell of baking wafting from inside explained the flour-covered apron she wore.

'Miss Wenlock? Doris Wenlock?'

She gave a cautious confirmation.

'I believe you know my friend, Henry Dyer?'

She pushed her fingers through her curly auburn hair, an attractive gesture. I could see what the workmen in the café had meant when describing her.

'Yes. Why?'

'You were with him on Saturday morning?'

'I may have been. Could you tell me what this is about, Mr…?'

'I apologise, Miss Wenlock. My name's James Given. Henry used to be my boss.' I explained why I was searching for him. 'Your name came up during my enquiries.'

The woman opened her front door wider. 'You'd better come in.'

She led me through to the kitchen and invited me to sit at her table. The aroma of bread was much stronger when she swung open the oven door to check her handiwork.

'I was with Mr Dyer on Saturday, Mr Given. I was doing a job for him and he wanted to meet to check on progress.'

'What sort of job?'

'I was arranging an anniversary party for him.'

'So why didn't you go to his house?'

'Because he intended to surprise his wife. They'll soon have been married forty years, a ruby wedding, and he wanted to do something special. He's booked a room at the Weston Manor Hotel, and I look after their catering. We were discussing the final numbers on his guest list.' She raised an eyebrow. 'I'm surprised you didn't know if you're a friend of his.'

'He'd not said anything to me about it.'

On the one hand I felt slighted, taking into account our recent contact, but this was overshadowed by my concern that Doris Wenlock's information indicated Henry hadn't simply walked away from his life and his wife. If he was planning a big celebration of their lifetime together, he'd hardly have upped sticks and made off.

'That's something I'll need to ask Henry about when I find him. How did he seem when you met?'

'As he always was. Polite. Businesslike. In a bit of a hurry, if I'm honest, and he kept apologising. He had that dog of his and it scratched around on the floor the whole time we were together. Mr Dyer said he was meeting someone later and he'd only brought Ben to give him some exercise.'

'He was meeting someone? Did he say who? Or where?'

Doris Wenlock paused for a moment, her eyes fixed on the tablecloth. 'I'm afraid he didn't. We finished our business and our tea, he paid me, and for the teas, and we left. I went to do some shopping and he walked in the other direction. I assumed he was going home. I do hope nothing's happened to him.'

'You said he paid you. For the catering?'

'Just a down payment, but it was a good few pounds. He planned for a lot of guests, so I needed some money up front to order the supplies. That's why I went to the shops as soon as I left Mr Dyer. I didn't like carrying so much cash on me. He said he'd settle the rest when he could get to the bank on the Monday.'

Again, if he'd been planning to leave, why would he have paid the woman a deposit, especially a big one? If his wife had known about the arrangements, then there might be some logic in pretending it was going ahead to put Audrey off the scent, but if he'd kept the party hidden, then it made no sense.

Miss Wenlock stopped and bit her bottom lip. 'I wondered why he hadn't contacted me. Does this mean I should stop making the arrangements, do you think? It would never do to prepare all the food and then have to cancel everything at the last minute.'

I said I didn't know what she should do for the best but suggested she might leave it for a few days if she could. I left her still pondering and wandered back to Audrey's to tell her what I'd found, leaving out that Henry had been organising a party. If he did turn up, he'd be none too pleased to find I'd let his secret out of the bag.

I went through Henry's morning route one more time with Audrey. She said she'd never been with him so couldn't be certain of every step, though she had a good idea. The way she described it, I wasn't looking forward to the long walk, my leg having become sore trekking behind Gleeson and then looking for the caterer's house.

The first section, around a mile, crossed over the river and then meandered through busy streets. It would have been unlikely for anything to happen to him there, in broad daylight, without it being noticed. My thigh began to throb when I reached the second half of Henry's walk, where he'd have crossed back over the river to enter the park. I sat for a break on the first bench I could find.

The parkland ran alongside the River Leam for several hundred yards, divided by a main road, with the Pump Rooms and bandstand on one side and Jephson Gardens, with its lake and nurseries, on the other. It would be impossible to search all of the grounds, even with a decent team of men, and there was sufficient shrubbery, trees and undergrowth round the sides to guarantee something could be hidden for days, if not weeks, on end. The lake and the river were other places where accidents, or crimes, might be hidden.

As I surveyed the park, trying to work out which way Henry might have crossed it, thunder rumbled in the distance. With the dog on its lead, he may have stuck to the paths, but they all had clear sight lines so any incident should have been spotted. Audrey had said the dog, Ben, had come home wearing his lead, so he hadn't escaped when running free on the grass. Again, any attack there would have been seen, so I could ignore the open spaces. I decided I'd begin a search along the shrubbery on the perimeter and use my walking stick to poke among the leaves. I'd covered about twenty feet by the path when lightning glinted off something on the ground, and a louder crack of thunder exploded overhead. I bent and picked up the blue and gold lapel badge revealed by the flash. It bore the name of Peel Chess Club. I popped it in my pocket to ask Audrey if she recognised it as belonging to Henry.

Before I could extend my search, the heavens opened, and I headed for cover in the pavilion, using a broken branch to mark where I'd found the badge. Several other walkers had followed my example and were sheltering from the storm.

One, a woman who looked to be in her early twenties and in service, rocked a pram and glanced at me leaning against the wall.

'Terrible day, isn't it?'

'Not a good day for a walk, that's for sure.'

'My mistress told me to bring baby William out for a walk, and I just knew I'd get drenched. She'll be so mad with me if I'm late back as well. Even worse if the young feller's soaked.'

To emphasise her dilemma, thunder banged again and the infant started to cry. I popped my head out to survey the clouds thinning to the west.

'Looks like it might blow over before long.' I held up my crossed fingers and the young nanny smiled.

'Let's hope so.'

We stayed with hailstones bouncing off the roof until the storm died away temporarily, allowing the woman and her charge to scurry away towards The Parade. The rest had allowed the ache in my leg to subside, so I went to resume my search. Within minutes, the heavy shower, contrary to my optimistic words, became a constant drizzle with low grey cloud stretching as far as I could see. I wasn't dressed for such weather and was tempted to go back to the house, though the badge I'd discovered meant I couldn't leave without looking further.

By the time I got back to my marker, I was so soaked I knew it could get no worse. I worked my way through the bushes towards the perimeter fence thirty feet from the path. It was drier under the canopy, though great blobs of rain dripped from the trees and splashed on my neck. Mounds of leaves, fallen over years, covered the ground and as I progressed I pushed them aside with my walking stick. Halfway in, between two substantial rhododendrons, I struck something solid. Solid but forgiving. A body, not a rock or tree stump.

I dropped to my knees and swept debris from the corpse with the back of my hand. I could tell it was Henry, even though he lay face-down. His size, frame and bald spot made it obvious. That bald spot framed a single gash at least an inch deep in his skull.

I turned him over and checked his pockets. His house keys, small change and fountain pen were all there. No wallet, nor the gold watch and chain he'd received when he'd retired. A quick search around the body didn't locate them. A robbery? But if a robbery, why leave the keys? All Henry's attacker would have had to do was watch his house, walk in through the front door when it was empty, and take what he wanted — lots more than his victim would have been carrying in the park. So perhaps the valuables had been stolen on impulse, after he'd laid Henry out. Did the assailant know he was dead?

I started to search for a weapon, then stopped. Rachel's voice whispered in my ear, telling me it wasn't my responsibility, and that I should leave it to the police. I did as I was told, and searched for the nearest telephone box instead.

ELEVEN

I hadn't expected to be meeting Inspector Moore again so soon, though this time we weren't in his office. He'd "invited" me to an interview room in the bowels of Leamington police station. It was like every other one I'd been in. Grey walls, four uncomfortable chairs, and a wooden table. Some of these places were in cellars, others on upper floors, wherever a spare room had been found which wasn't needed for anything else. The worst ones had no windows; claustrophobic spaces from which both coppers and villains alike wanted to get out of as soon as possible. This one had a single barred window high up on one wall, making it at least a step up from those.

By Moore's side was a younger man, who he introduced as Sergeant Derek Templar. Templar's brown suit gave no indication of his rank, one of the perks of plainclothes detectives. The black patch over his left eye gave him an excuse for not being on active duty overseas.

'You say you were looking for him, Mr Given?' said Inspector Moore. 'Why there?'

'Because his wife suggested he might have gone that way on the day he disappeared.'

'Did you search every nook and cranny all along the route, then?'

'No, of course not. It would have taken days.'

'So why there?'

I shook my head. 'Come on, Inspector, you know how it works. I followed my nose. I discarded the places it couldn't have been done, and concentrated on those where it could.'

'And it just happened to take you directly to a body. Damn sensitive nose, that. They must miss you over in Kenilworth.'

'It didn't take me straight to Henry. I walked the way he'd have gone, keeping my eyes peeled for anywhere he might have been concealed.'

'You knew he was dead, then?'

'No. I was hoping you were right and he'd gone on a jaunt with a younger woman. But I spoke to the lady he was seen with; Doris Wenlock is her name. You could have spoken to her as well if you'd bothered to look, and their meeting was perfectly innocent. She was arranging an anniversary party for Henry and his wife. When she told me, I became more concerned for his welfare than I had been.'

Moore smirked. 'That's nice. So you went to the park. Big park, that. What made you look where you did? I've been down there, and you can't see the spot where you found him from the path.'

'Are you joking? If he'd been visible, then someone would have found him before me. Enough people walk through there every day.' I pulled the chess club badge from my pocket and showed him. 'And I'm a detective, or at least I was, not a pen-pusher. I found this on the edge of the undergrowth. Henry had told me he'd taken up chess since retiring, and I thought it might have been his. I was going to ask Audrey when I got back. Has anybody told her yet?'

Moore took the badge from me, inspected it and tossed it on the desk. 'That's not your problem, is it? You need to worry about yourself.'

'In what way?'

'You shouldn't need me to spell it out for you, if you're such a great detective. You turn up in town, at the invitation of your old boss, you say, and next thing he's dead in a park. What's to say you didn't have some kind of a grudge, and came over to Leamington and confronted ex-Superintendent Dyer? Maybe you struggled and it all got out of hand. Then you concoct a story of looking for him, even coming to see me to make it seem realistic.'

I snorted. 'Well, you've some imagination there, Inspector.' I glanced at Templar, who squirmed at being caught in the crossfire. 'What do you think, Sergeant? Should write books, shouldn't he?' I turned back to Moore. 'Audrey Dyer telephoned and asked me to come.'

'Well, she would, wouldn't she? She'd been to see us, and we'd told her we couldn't do anything for a few days. Standard procedure — which you'd have known. She was obviously going to call on her husband's friend, a retired detective. Makes sense.'

'Have you an inkling what this so-called grudge might have been? No, you haven't, because there wasn't one. You haven't even asked me where I was on the day Henry went missing. Sloppy.'

'I'll give you sloppy. I haven't asked because there's no point. You're not a stupid man, Given. If you planned to get rid of Henry Dyer, for whatever reason, you'd have made sure you had an alibi set up in advance. Just in case.'

I'd seen police officers work this way many times in the past. On the one hand, he'd argued that it was a confrontation which had escalated, then he'd said that I'd planned it to the finest of details. Anything to fit the decision he'd made. Moore could already see his boss's smiles when he handed them such a quick result.

'I can't argue with your logic there, Inspector, but you give me more credit for intelligence than I have. As I said, you've some imagination. I could never have dreamed up a plot like that. On Monday morning, when Henry left home, I was at work thirty miles away in Birmingham.'

'And I expect you've a dozen witnesses.'

'I have. But tell me this. If I had killed Henry and, even if me coming to see you earlier was camouflage, why would I then pretend to find the body then inform the police? You weren't looking for him, so there'd be no point. He could have lain under those trees for weeks, even months, certainly long enough for him to be unrecognisable. If you'd found him in that state, even if you could identify him you'd have no idea when he died, and you'd have nothing to connect me to his death.'

Moore's assistant grinned as if I had a point, which vanished when Moore swung round. The sergeant spluttered and tried to regain ground with his boss. 'This is nonsense, Given. You've already told us you work for your father, a Jew, I believe. He'd be bound to lie for you if you asked him, wouldn't he? Your kind always stick together. You could easily have gone in early, let a few of the others see you, then slipped out unseen and have been here in an hour. You met your victim in the park, bashed him over the head and was back home again by lunchtime.'

I looked him in the eye. 'All of that is perfectly plausible, Sergeant, but it's pure conjecture, not evidence.' I turned back to Moore. 'Unless you are going to charge me, I think we're about finished. When I came in, I'd hoped you might want to find Henry's killer rather than jumping at the first option which came your way. Now I can see I was wrong and will have to look for him myself. When I bring you the evidence, I still have a few friends on the force who'll be interested to hear you didn't want to bother investigating.'

Moore puffed out his cheeks, then asked Templar to leave us for a few minutes. When he'd gone, the inspector leant back in his chair, folded his arms and groaned. 'I'm sorry, Mr Given, this was the last thing I wanted. When they invited me back to fill a gap, I didn't expect to have a murder land on my desk. For most of my career before I retired, I sat in an office preparing minor cases for court. I only got the rank because there were a few coppers working under me. When you turned up, I had a body, a murder scene, and someone who knew the victim. The obvious thing to do was to make a connection. You'd be the clearest suspect. Admittedly, you being a police inspector made it a bit less likely, but you have to admit, I had to start somewhere.'

'You're right there, Inspector. Especially as you agreed I could look around to see if I could find anything. I will concede your last point, though. You did have to start somewhere. So where do we go from here? Are you going to charge me?'

He laughed. 'Not today. Our doctor will continue to look at Dyer and see what he can figure out. I'll go and have a word with the wife to fill in the blanks, then ask a few questions around town in case anyone has seen or heard anything. We'll take it from there.'

'Is it all right if I keep digging? I won't tread on your toes, and I'll pass on anything I think is relevant.'

'Can I stop you?'

'Probably not.'

'Then you'd better get on with it. I'll have a word with the higher-ups to see what help we can give you.'

TWELVE

Back at the house, Audrey's puffy, red-rimmed eyes told of her tears, even though she'd gathered herself to answer the door. They'd sent a raw young constable to give her the news, and he'd almost broken down himself. The least they could have done was send a more senior man, someone with a bit of experience in these matters. She'd been provided with no details, only that someone found her husband's body and a suspect was "helping with enquiries". From this she'd worked out Henry had been murdered, rather than an accident or suicide, but that's all she had.

I filled her in on where I'd found him, and she confirmed the badge was his. She'd held some hope his killer had been apprehended, until I explained I'd been the one the police had hauled in to answer questions. Audrey showed the look of loss I'd seen so many times on the faces of relatives of murder victims.

'Why, James? Why would anyone do this to my Henry?'

This was the question they always asked, and I never had an answer. The best I could do was try to offer some hope. To her and to me.

'We'll find out, Audrey. The police are on it now, and I'll do everything I can to help them. Can anyone come to stay with you for a few days?'

Audrey had a sister in the north who she'd already rung, but she couldn't get to Leamington until the next day. I said I'd stay overnight and follow up on a few things in the morning, but I needed to get back to Birmingham by lunchtime. We spent what was left of the afternoon making funeral arrangements, and Audrey wrote to, or telephoned, all their friends to convey the news. Around four o'clock, Bob Moore rang and questioned Audrey for about quarter of an hour, then asked if she could go in to the station the next day to make a formal statement.

I rang my father which, despite his condolences, didn't go well once he learnt I'd be away for at least the next morning. Rachel was more sympathetic, though she had a brittleness which told me she was not impressed with me becoming involved.

'I'm sorry, Rachel, but you wouldn't want me to leave Audrey in this state, surely?'

'Of course not. It isn't the extra night away that's bothering me, it's you getting in deep again.'

'I'm not getting in deep. I've told you I've handed over to the local police, which is what I said I'd do. They don't want me to leave the area just yet, and I've a few loose ends to tie up tomorrow morning. Then I'll be home. Promise.'

Rachel sighed. I could tell she didn't believe me. When I hung up, I wasn't sure I believed me either.

I joined Audrey in the sitting room and asked her to take me through what she'd told Moore.

'He didn't ask me much, just when I'd last seen Henry and if I could think of anyone who might want to harm him. I told him what I'd told you, James, that there was no-one coming to mind other than the possibility of someone he'd prosecuted. Inspector Moore said that was unlikely with Henry being desk-based for so long.'

'You said Henry didn't seem his usual self before he went out that morning?'

'Well, there was something going on — nothing I could put my finger on. He seemed in good humour but a bit detached. When I asked him about it, he said it was nothing — just that he'd met someone from his past and was trying to make sense of it.'

'Did he say who?'

'No. Only that it was somebody he hadn't expected to bump into in Leamington.'

'Why didn't you mention this to me before?'

'I'm sorry, James. It didn't seem important until you just asked me. When we talked before, Henry was only missing. Not…'

The poor woman broke down again. I dug out the brandy bottle and poured a large measure. She took it in shaking hands and threw down a gulp, resulting in a coughing fit. After it had subsided, she laid the glass on a coffee table and rubbed her eyes with her palms.

I gave her another moment before returning to my question. 'You're sure Henry didn't mention anyone's name? A man? A woman?'

'Not as far as I can recall. I don't think I even asked him. Do you think this person might have been the one who … who murdered Henry?'

'Possibly, Audrey. I don't know, but you should mention it to Inspector Moore when you see him tomorrow.'

I didn't tell her I might know who Henry had met. There'd be time enough for that when I'd had a word with him.

I'd had nothing to eat since the scone in the café and I was starving, so I offered to make supper for Audrey, thinking she'd be in no frame of mind to cook.

She shook her head. 'Not at all, James. It will take my mind off all this for a while. Just give me ten minutes and I'll have something ready.'

True to her word, she called me through to the kitchen for a feast of cold beef and salad. She picked at hers while I tried not to wolf mine down. When we'd finished and I'd stacked the dishes in the sink, she served up apple pie and custard.

'You're a wonder, Audrey.'

'Not really. I'd cooked it all in case Henry came home today.'

The tears then came and stayed with her, on and off, until we both turned in at about half past nine.

THIRTEEN

Thursday 18th July, 1940

Next morning, I left after breakfast with two jobs lined up before I needed to catch my train home. The first was to look again at the spot where I'd found Henry, the second was to track down Terry Gleeson.

At the entrance to the park, I bumped into Bob Moore.

'Any progress, Inspector?' Our last encounter had left us too far apart for first names, which was a shame because I liked him.

'I've just been back to the scene. Nothing to give much of a clue about what happened. The wife told me he'd no enemies so, with the wallet and watch being gone, it seems to me it was just a random attack. He's walking through the back end of the park, looks like he might have a pound or two, and some villain jumps him.'

'In broad daylight and with no-one noticing? How many other attacks have there been in here?'

Moore flushed slightly. 'None, as far as I'm aware.'

'Don't you think there would have been if some toerag had found a good place to jump passers-by? And Henry was a big man. Not easy to put down.'

'If he was surprised then he'd have been off his guard. There are signs of a scuffle on the edge of the trees further down, probably where the attack happened, and Dyer could have been pushed out of sight then cracked over the head.'

'Maybe, though I have my doubts. I think he met someone he knew and they stepped behind the bushes so as not to be seen. Audrey told me last night that Henry had recently bumped into someone from his past. She'll tell you when you take her statement later.'

'Any idea who?'

'I've an idea, but I don't want to say anything until I'm sure. I'm checking after I go from here. Anything from the medical examination?'

'Not yet. I'll let you know when I hear something. Where will I reach you?'

I told him I intended on catching the train home later in the morning, and gave him my number in Birmingham. Before Moore walked away, he apologised again for questioning me. I told him to forget it and that I'd have done the same in his position. Not entirely true, but it seemed better to keep him on side and supplying me with information. I waited a few minutes until he was out of sight, then wandered down to where Henry's body had been.

It was clear the police had been there, flattening the leaves and grass all around. I'd read an article once about how the victim, the perpetrator and the investigator all left traces of themselves at a crime scene, and how important it was for the police to disturb as little as possible. It seemed unfortunate that Bob Moore's boys hadn't read the same piece.

I took a pencil and my notepad from my pocket, and drew a rough sketch of the area I intended to search, drawing a matchstick man where I'd found Henry's body. I paced the length along the path, and the depth from path to fence, marking the position of two large trees on the sketch. I looked at the place where Moore had said there'd been a scuffle, but I could see no evidence of activity between there and where the victim lay, so I discounted it as not connected. I extended my search, criss-crossing the entire area well beyond where the police had trodden everything down, making sure I flicked piles of leaves over, rather than standing on them. About ten yards away, I found something the police had missed, partly because I'd expected it to be in the vicinity. A brown leather wallet. Inside were a good number of crisp banknotes and several papers. There could be no doubt it was Henry's.

So the motive hadn't been robbery. I marked my plan where I'd made the discovery and slipped the wallet into my jacket pocket, then continued my search.

I spent another three-quarters of an hour looking, but still didn't find Henry's gold watch and chain. I'd thought the robbery had been faked as a smokescreen and the valuables dumped, but perhaps the thief had been disturbed and, in his hurry to get away, he'd dropped the wallet and not noticed. Unsure about my next steps if that was true, I double-checked my measurements and moved on to my second task of the morning.

The outside of the Argyll Hotel looked no more affluent than it had on my last visit. From the doorway of an empty building across the street, I kept an eye on the entrance, as well as both directions. The hotel's neighbours were just as down-market. Shabby grocers, greengrocers, butchers, and hardware shops attracted a stream of poorly dressed individuals wearing glum expressions. I was watching a pair of these, an elderly man and woman, who'd started a conversation on the pavement, when the door of Gleeson's accommodation twitched open and I had to duck back. A man, short, bearded and dressed in trousers and a shirt several sizes too big, stood on the step and peered up and down the road. Seeing nothing to hold his attention, he walked to the gutter and spat, then lit a cigarette and ambled away. I watched his progress until he slipped into a pub, which would barely have been open for five minutes.

I didn't have to wait much longer for Terry Gleeson to come out. My former colleague strode the opposite way to his predecessor, along the street in the direction of the station. For a moment I thought he might be leaving Leamington, then noticed his lack of luggage. Hanging back until he had a good lead, I followed him for five minutes before he turned into a tearoom in the shadow of a railway bridge. From across the street, I could see he'd sat on his own and settled with a drink and his newspaper. Other than the woman behind the counter, I could only make out one other person inside.

A bell rattled above the door when I entered, and without looking at Gleeson I took a table on the opposite side of the room. From the corner of my eye I could tell he was watching me, but I pretended to ignore him until the waitress brought my order. Then I straightened my back and made a great show of looking around the room, screwing up my eyes to focus when I spotted him.

'Terry? Terry Gleeson? Is that you?'

He scowled and raised a hand in acknowledgement. 'Given.' The single word made me wonder if he'd spotted me one of the times I'd followed him, and so expected me to appear at some point. I lifted my cup and saucer and carried them over to where he was sitting.

'Mind if I join you?'

'It's a free country.'

'I expect it still is, at least for most people. Speaking of which, I thought you might be in prison by now.'

'Pfft. Why would I be?'

'Come on, Terry, you know and I know you stuck a knife in someone.'

'Not that I'm admitting anything, but the man was scum and no-one would be bothered by his passing. You of all people should be grateful. He'd have done for you if I hadn't got to him first.'

'That's true, but it wouldn't have stopped me putting you away for his murder if I had the proof.'

'So what are you doing over here, Given? I heard you live in Birmingham now?'

'I might ask you the same thing. Isn't Coventry your stomping ground?'

'Not that it's any of your business, but I'm visiting a friend.'

'That's nice.' I wasn't going to mess about catching up on old times. 'Speaking of friends, did you hear Henry Dyer has been found dead? Hardly ten minutes' walk from here.'

I didn't know how good an actor Gleeson was, but he either beat the best in the West End theatres, or he genuinely didn't know Henry had been killed. He shook his head and took a drink from his cup. 'What? Dyer? How?'

'I was hoping you'd be able to tell me, Terry.'

'What's that supposed to mean?'

'I'm told the boss met an old acquaintance before he was killed, and it had been bothering him. Was it you?'

Gleeson stood and pushed back his chair, almost toppling it to the floor. 'I'll tell you what, Given, why don't you just get lost and mind your own business? I'm sorry to hear about Dyer, but I've nothing to say to you. You're not even a copper anymore.'

Without waiting for a reply, Gleeson slurped the dregs of his tea, banged some change on the table and stormed out of the café. As the bell on the door faded, I smiled and shrugged at the waitress and customers staring at the scene open-mouthed. Getting under Gleeson's skin had given me much more pleasure than it should have done, and I looked forward to following up our little chat in the not-too-distant future.

When I arrived back at his workshop, my father asked me to join him upstairs. I followed him, and Mama fussed for a few minutes, made us tea and a sandwich each, then kept out of the way when my father took me through to the parlour. Much smaller than the living room and the kitchen, the space was carpeted and cosy, but in a man's way. There were deep brown armchairs and a wooden fire surround holding mementos of his life in Russia, including a photograph I'd kept above my desk in Kenilworth and returned to him before moving to France. Thatched hovels, a muddy, rutted road, and the family. I focused on this picture, waiting for him to start.

'It won't do, you know, Jacob. You said you'd be back yesterday and now here you are, a day late and the work piling up.'

As if to emphasise his point, his clock chimed half past one. My father glanced at it and shook his head. 'See, Jacob, that is the whole morning gone.'

'I'm sorry, Papa, something came up.'

'And did this something pay your wages for the day? Did this something send a person over here to do your jobs?'

I hung my head and waited for him to continue.

'No, I didn't think so. I've tried to be understanding. God knows I have. But it can't go on. Either you're working for me or you're an amateur detective, I don't think you can have it both ways.'

'I'm not an amateur, Papa.'

'Well, you're not getting paid, for sure. That makes you an amateur in my book.'

The sore he'd been picking at over the last year was about to be exposed again.

'I'll never understand why you left the police, Jacob. It was not my choice of career for you, but at least you were good at it. And it paid well. Now you're here and not wanting to be. If I'm honest, it feels like you are taking advantage.'

'That's not fair. I've taken a couple of days off, and I'll make up the time now I'm back. You know I will. Have I ever let you down?' As soon as I spoke, I knew he'd give me an answer I didn't want to hear.

'Not over this.'

I sat for a moment, letting his comment sink in. 'What do you mean?'

'Nothing.'

'It isn't "nothing", Papa, is it? So what did you mean?'

My father rocked back in his armchair, sighed and folded his arms.

'You ran away. Never a word, just packed a few things and left us. Me and your Mama. Not a word for weeks. We had no idea where you'd gone, then you write from some port telling us you're working on boats. And a good job waiting here for you.'

'Twenty years and you're still holding on to that? Have you never figured out that's why I left? I didn't want to spend my days cutting cloth and sewing stitches. I wanted something else.'

'So you're saying my life wasn't good enough for you? You're above all of that?'

I stood, shaking. 'If that's what you think, Papa, then there's no more to say. But once again you're making it about you, and what you want, not what I want.'

'And where are you now, my son? You've seen the world, you've been a big grand policeman and got yourself half-killed — more than once — and still you came back to me when you wanted to put food on the table. Huh.'

I didn't give him the dignity of an answer. Instead, I slammed the door and stormed down the stairs to my desk.

The remainder of the afternoon flew past, and by its end two days' paperwork had been read, dealt with, filed or binned, without my temper abating in the least. My father knew well enough to stay away.

At five o'clock, all the tailors and seamstresses went home. My father turned off the light above his table and climbed the stairs to join the family for the evening meal. I picked up the telephone.

My first call was to Rachel to tell her I'd be a little late. She listened and gave non-committal responses, but I wasn't in the mood for another argument so I just hung up when I'd finished. My second call was to Bob Moore. I told him I'd found Henry's wallet with its contents complete, so, in my opinion, robbery didn't seem to be the motive for his murder. He wasn't happy I'd not taken the evidence to him straight away. Moore had every right to be annoyed, I would have been if the boot had been on the other foot. An apology was in order.

'I'm sorry, Inspector. I had other things to do, then needed to get back to work.'

I wasn't sure my explanation satisfied him, but he accepted it with good grace.

'Are you sure it's his, James?'

So, we were now on first-name terms. Perhaps he'd begun to appreciate my refusal to let go.

'There were personal papers in it. No doubt it belonged to Henry.'

'Then perhaps someone came along, and the thief panicked and dropped it when he ran.'

'The same thing occurred to me, Bob, but how long would it have taken for him to pick it up?'

'Maybe he didn't notice.'

'Well, he'd have noticed soon enough; he'd attacked someone to steal it. Even if he'd been disturbed, why didn't he come back to look for it when the coast was clear?'

'The place was swarming with police. He'd have been stupid to do such a thing.'

'There were no police there until after I'd found the body, two days later. The killer had plenty of time to go back. You and your boys were hardly discreet; he'd have seen them a mile off. Still, you seem to have made your mind up about this, Bob, so I'll send the wallet over and you can look for fingerprints. See if anything turns up.'

'It's not just me who thinks this, you know. Our doctor has taken a look. Says death occurred from a single blow. Something heavy, but not a frenzied attack. Most likely intended to knock Mr Dyer out, not kill him.'

I asked if he'd any indication of what had been used.

'Not yet. "Significant force," the doc has said. Found the wound to be deep when he cleaned it up. Cracked the victim's skull and bruised the brain. Would have been rendered unconscious straight away.'

'Any thoughts on when it happened?'

I heard Moore flip through papers.

'Says the weather, hot one minute and the temperature dropping and pouring down the next, makes it difficult to pin down. He also said, in the shade under the trees, there'd be more creepy-crawlies around than on open ground, so they got to work more quickly. Doc's best guess is that our man died sometime on Monday morning. That seems to fit with what we know of his movements.'

'Thank God for that. I'd hate to think he'd been lying there for a couple of days still breathing when we could have been looking for him properly.' I hadn't meant for this to sound like a reproach on the police's lack of willingness to roll up their sleeves and take Audrey's concerns seriously, but Moore didn't seem impressed.

'You know well enough, James, my hands were tied. We were faced with a grown man who'd hardly been gone five minutes. If I'd committed officers to a full-scale search, then Dyer had turned up on the arm of a floozy, I'd have been a laughingstock, and hauled over the coals by my boss to boot.'

'I know, I know, Bob. I didn't mean anything by it. I didn't rush over when Audrey rang either. I also told her to give it a day or two.'

If the medical evidence had shown Henry had been alive for a while after the attack, I'd never have forgiven myself.

When I hung up on Bob Moore, the sun had dipped behind the surrounding buildings. The workshop had settled in shade, and being alone in its quietness gave me more peace than I'd felt for weeks. I took a few moments to savour it, the solid ticking of the wall clock, which I never usually heard amidst the usual din of business, only emphasising the serenity. My father sometimes spent an evening on his own down here, and was always at his table an hour before anyone else arrived, and I wondered if this was why. A space of his own. No distractions, no reminders of his family responsibilities.

I let it hang over me until thoughts of Henry's murder surfaced again. I'd found no motive, and without a motive the path to a solution was hidden. Bob Moore's theory of robbery didn't hold water, and the only person I knew who was connected with Henry's past was Terry Gleeson.

I rang my ex-colleague in Kenilworth, Phil Trimble, who'd known Gleeson. Even though it was late, Phil was still at the station. We chatted for a few minutes, catching up on news, and I asked if he'd heard about Henry Dyer.

'I did, James. Terrible. It's all over the station. I hear you were the one found him.'

'Terrible's right, Phil. Poor man hardly retired five minutes ago. He and Audrey were hoping to spend his retirement years together. She's devastated.'

'Do the lads over there have any idea who did it?'

'Not at present, and not likely to have one the way they're going on. That's part of the reason I'm phoning. What do you know of the local inspector, Bob Moore? You worked together for a while, didn't you?'

'I was his sergeant for a few months, years back. Why?'

'It's just that I think he's being a bit easy-going. Left the force and came back due to the war, but now he wants a quiet life. He's settled on Henry's death being a robbery gone wrong and is proving hard to move from there.'

Phil Trimble was one of the nicest of men. Always wanting to see the best in people, so I knew I'd need to pick over whatever he told me about Moore, but I'd had to ask.

'As I said, James, I knew him a long time ago. When I did, he was a good copper. Not sharp, like you, but steady. Keen to get a result and wouldn't let go of a case until he'd got one. I can't say he hasn't changed, but at the time I bet you'd have got on with him. Does that help?'

'It does, thanks. Can I ask you something else?'

'Sure, what else do you need?'

'Terry Gleeson. Heard anything about him recently?'

'Not much since he left. Rumour was he planned to go to America when he got his pension, then he'd try to get a place with the police over there.'

'What prevented him? He's still in England, isn't he?'

'Didn't you hear? His pension was held up, pending appeal, and without it he'd not got the cash to see him through until he was settled.'

'Held up? How?'

'The super had it stopped. After you left, Henry thought some more about what Gleeson had done. He'd not enough evidence to take him to trial, but he whispered a word in the chief constable's ear and Gleeson was retired. He had no job, a threat of no references, and a recommendation for no pension.'

When I arrived home from work, later than I'd intended, I told Rachel what Phil Trimble had said, then went to telephone Bob Moore to fill him in about Gleeson, but she stopped me.

'Surely you're not carrying on at this time of night, James? You're already late enough this evening.'

I sighed. 'I'm sorry. It will only take five minutes.'

'Well, that's five minutes too long. Don't you think you should pay at least a little attention to me? It's not fair.'

'I know it's not, and I've already apologised. What else do you want me to do?'

'Don't make the phone call.'

'It's not that simple, and you know it. There are so many loose ends, and I need to get Moore working on them.'

Rachel folded her arms and turned away. 'When will you grasp that you're not a policeman any longer, James? I'm sure you had your fair share of unsolved crimes, so is this how it's going to be? Whenever a past acquaintance contacts you, or a new piece of evidence comes to light, you're going to charge off in your own time … in *our* time … and play the knight in shining armour? Well, I'm fed-up with it.'

I tried to put my arms round her, but she shrugged me off and went into the other room. There was no arguing. She was right. In my last couple of years in the police I couldn't wait to get out, fed-up with all the horror and pain. Despite this, the habit of solving puzzles had become ingrained, and that's all it was: a habit. I might have liked to dress it up as a sense of justice, but really that had only ever applied to one case. When that had been put to bed, I'd felt free to leave. I decided not to make the phone call. It would do no harm to wait to build a stronger case against Gleeson.

Regardless, Rachel and I shared another frosty night, which hung over all the next day, so I made doubly sure over the weekend that I paid full attention to her, taking us on a bus ride to the botanical gardens on Saturday with an afternoon tea afterwards. We seemed to be friends again by the end of it. On Sunday, after lunch, we went through the week's papers again, still with no success on the house front.

The next few days dragged by. Every morning and afternoon, my father hovered around my desk, either bored or not trusting me with the job in hand, I wasn't sure which. Before long, I'd be forced to have it out with him.

There was little for me, or him, to do. Everyone in the workshop knew their job inside out, so they needed little direction, and we had plenty of work with orders continuing to come in. Our only real difficulty might have been obtaining fabric, with so much being commandeered for the war effort, but we had good stocks and enough friends in the trade to keep problems to a minimum. I began to suspect the only reason he fussed was because he knew his retirement couldn't be far away, and he wanted to make sure the business would pass into a safe pair of hands. This would be another illusion I'd need to dispel for him.

If the constant interruptions weren't enough to keep my mind off my work, I couldn't get the conversation with Phil Trimble out of my head.

Before I'd left the police, Henry had ranted that he wanted to kick Gleeson out with nothing. I never believed he'd actually go through with it.

Would this be enough of a motive for murder? Gleeson may have been as bent as a paperclip, and had shown his willingness to use extreme violence, but that was on a villain. Would he chance taking revenge on a senior police officer, retired or not? On the other hand, Audrey had said Henry had met someone from his past who'd disturbed him, and the caterer, Doris Wenlock, had said he'd planned to meet someone after he left her. Could Gleeson and Henry have met on Saturday and again on that Monday morning? Did Terry Gleeson murder Henry during an argument, then steal his wallet and watch to cover it up? If I'd still had my warrant card, I'd have pulled him in and asked him, and all week I wished I'd asked Bob Moore to do it.

FOURTEEN

Thursday 25th July, 1940

Audrey Dyer telephoned me at home on Wednesday evening to tell me Henry would be buried on Friday. Another day off needed, and my father would be livid. I suspected I'd not get an easy ride from Rachel either, so I decided I'd tell her nothing until I'd discussed it with my father.

He had hardly spoken to me since our spat the previous week, and I'd not been inclined to try to break the ice. If we'd exchanged words at all, it was either related to work or in my mother's presence, and even then it was never more than the bare minimum. I approached him on Thursday, just before I left for the night. He'd been tidying his table when I walked over to tell him I'd not be in the next day. For a minute he ignored me, as if he hadn't heard, then he sat on his stool and glared.

'Not another one, Jacob?'

'It's a funeral. I can't not go.'

'But you've had so much time off recently. Can you not just send your apologies?'

'No, I can't. Henry was my boss and I respected him.'

'And what if I refuse?'

I stared at him. 'I'm not actually asking your permission, Papa. I'm going and I'll see you on Monday. If I'm back.'

He opened his mouth as if to answer, but I turned and went back to my desk, then slipped on my jacket and left.

When I arrived home, Rachel expressed even more annoyance than my father had when I said I'd be going to

Leamington for the funeral, and there were some things I wanted to do there over the weekend.

My wife's music school was beginning to build back up again, and this kept her occupied some of the time. Before we'd gone to France she'd had quite an enterprise, busy most evenings, teaching classes in one or two schools and directing a local, though prestigious, choir. Rachel wanted to get back to this level, believing music was more important than ever in wartime, but she wanted to keep numbers down for the time being in case we moved out of the city. As a result, she was left to her own devices when I was in Leamington, and she didn't like it.

'It's getting beyond a joke, James. I don't enjoy being left here on my own, you know.'

'Then come with me.'

'What would be the point? I hardly knew the man. I'd be at a funeral surrounded by strangers, then you'd be off on your adventures all weekend, leaving me God knows where.'

'Adventures? You make it sound like I enjoy this.'

My wife laughed bitterly. 'Enjoy? You absolutely relish it, James. Sometimes I wonder why you ever left the police in the first place.'

'You know why. Because I couldn't stand it any longer, because you wanted me to, and so I could be with you.'

'That sounds so noble. We both know the real reason was because you were injured and couldn't do it anymore. As for wanting to be with me, in France you were off with that young woman half the time, and now you're away at Audrey Dyer's beck and call.'

Rachel's accusation stung. We'd argued about Marie-Clair more than once, but I'd hoped she'd seen there was nothing to it, just me doing my best to help someone to achieve the career they wanted. Marie-Clair had wanted to become a detective, so I'd let her assist me on a murder case. I found it hard to believe Rachel would now be jealous of Audrey Dyer, a woman almost twice her age.

'I'm not at Audrey's "beck and call", as you put it. Her husband has been murdered, the police don't seem that interested, and I might be able to help. In Brittany you pressed me as hard as Marie-Clair did to do my best to find who murdered that poor woman.'

Rachel came back from the sink and stood over me at the table. She was trembling. 'Well, I don't think you should go. I've nearly lost you twice in the last year, and I couldn't stand it happening again. If you're going to persist in putting yourself in danger, then we'll need to think about our future together.'

If she'd slapped me in the face it would have stung less.

'What? You'll give up our marriage if I go ahead with this? Is that what you're saying?'

Rachel drew a deep breath. 'I'm sorry, James, I think that *is* what I'm saying. When you came out of the police force, I was so pleased. We were going to have a good life together. You and me, somewhere in the countryside. No crime, no possibility of me getting a call one night to say you'd been injured, or worse. But you don't seem satisfied with a vision of us growing older together. And if you're not, then I don't know what we'll do.'

I stood and she backed away, but I took a step towards her, wanting to take her in my arms and tell her it would all be fine. The steel in her eyes told me to keep my distance. Instead, I did the stupidest thing imaginable. I shrugged my shoulders, left her to the washing up, and made the bed up in our spare room.

The rest of my evening was spent up there with a book, listening to Rachel hammering through her piano scales in the room below. We didn't speak until I made a hot drink before going to bed, and even then it was a sullen "goodnight" from me, with no reply from Rachel. I plodded off upstairs, then tossed and turned the whole night through, replaying our argument inside my head.

Next morning, I left the house by eight, with a note propped on the mantelpiece telling Rachel I'd see her on Saturday evening. I strolled to Moor Street station. Early shoppers in the city centre scurried in and out of stores, like so many ants, gathering food and other necessaries for the days ahead. Another ordinary day, unless you heard the newspaper vendors on street corners shouting the latest headlines, all of them about death, destruction and politician's statements.

By half past nine, I was pushing my breakfast around a plate in the Leamington station buffet, dreading the rest of the morning, and planning the visits I'd make over the two days.

I met Audrey at her house then followed the procession to the cemetery chapel, where we hurried inside to get out of the rain as soon as it was decent to do so. As I took in the sombre dress and the solemn service, I was reminded of the same occasions in my Jewish faith. Of how I, in the same way, alongside my parents, would have stood grieving silently when my brother, Ariel, had been laid to rest, if we'd a body to bury. He'd been killed in Spain, fighting in a war he'd believed in, and he'd been buried there, like hundreds of other foreign soldiers.

The morning had broken with heavy low cloud and persistent drizzle, and by the time we'd walked down to the graveside, a northerly wind scythed through the mourners. For some reason, all the cemeteries I'd ever been to were in exposed spots, either hillsides or open fields. The Leamington one was large, and the surrounding trees provided no protection. The mourners, every one in black, pulled their coats tightly around them whenever they thought they were out of the vicar's sight. Alec Kendrick joined us at the graveside as the vicar dropped the first handfuls of earth on the coffin and offered a final prayer for Henry's soul. The latecomer caught Audrey's eye and mouthed "sorry". Unlike everyone else's black, he wore a brown business suit under a grey gaberdine, so I suspected he'd come straight from his factory.

The best the force could do was send a chief superintendent and allow one or two of Henry's old colleagues an hour off to pay their respects. All of these left as soon as the formalities were over. Even Bob Moore didn't turn up. It struck me that Henry would have had a much better send-off if he'd died in service — an assistant chief constable and a guard of honour at least.

Audrey stood silently by the grave as people began to depart, her stillness more moving than if she'd collapsed in tears. Her sister touched her elbow, whispered a few words in her ear, then began to shepherd mourners towards the waiting cars which would take them to a hall where sandwiches, tea and cakes would be served. This attempt at normality in the midst of grief — a soulless room with steel beams, cream-painted walls and trestle tables — lacked all the cosiness and intimacy one would hope for at the passing of a loved one.

I found myself in a corner between the refreshments and the toilet door, chatting to a heavily built man, Daniel Prentice, in a dark waist-coated suit. He told me he'd been Henry's bank manager.

'Known him for years, more or less since he opened his account. Oh yes, an extremely nice man. Frugal and managed his money well. Never an overdraft or a loan needed. Good golfer, too.'

'You played with him?'

'Once a week over the last couple of years, not so much before. D'you play yourself, Mr Given?'

'Never. Sorry. I can see the fascination, though — plenty of time out of doors and a good companion.'

'Indeed. You should take it up. Get yourself some clubs and a few lessons. Make a new man of you.'

'Maybe I will. When did you last play with Henry?'

'Not since the course closed. Damned war.'

'So you've not seen him for a while?'

'Goodness me, yes. Saw him the day he was killed. Came into the bank in the morning. Didn't speak to him, but I waved. The counter clerk came to see me because Henry wanted a decent sum out in cash and I had to authorise it.'

'Substantial?'

'Well, in cash, yes. Much more than he'd take out most weeks. Apparently he'd said he had to pay the balance of a bill to a caterer and was buying a special present for his wife.'

'What time was this?'

'I'd think about quarter past eleven. With the clerk coming to see me, I'd guess Henry would have been with us about ten minutes, perhaps fifteen.' The bank manager shook his head. 'I do wish I'd made the time to go out and have a word with him. Perhaps none of this would have happened if he'd been later.'

I told him I didn't think it would have made much difference, though this was largely to make him feel better. His revelation that Henry had withdrawn money on the morning of his death to buy Audrey an anniversary present added even more sadness to his passing. It made me recognise how life was fleeting, and how I should do everything I could to spend what time I had with Rachel. His recollection also changed the timing of the morning. Henry hadn't mentioned to Audrey that he was going to the bank; it would have given the game away. But it would have added twenty to thirty minutes to his walk and the place where he met his death.

Across the room, Alec Kendrick came in, raised a hand in recognition, then walked over to join us. He shook Prentice's hand.

'You've met Mr Given, then, Dan. Good man, knows his stuff. If you ever need a detective, give him a call.'

The bank manager laughed and said he'd bear it in mind. The two talked about golf and handicaps for a few moments in the stilted way people do at these events before Prentice looked at his watch and said he'd need to get back to work. 'Need to keep the world turning, you know. Nice talking to you.'

When he walked away, Kendrick cursed.

'Pompous fool. It's the likes of me and my factory that make the money. Men like him just guard it and charge us an arm and a leg for the privilege.'

I spluttered at his candour. 'You're not keen on banks, then?'

'Not at all, James — it is all right to call you James?'

'Of course.'

'Most bank managers are like hell and damnation vicars, lecturing you on the perils of borrowing when you need a loan to build the business, then rattling the collection plate for you to deposit when you've made a bob or two. I wouldn't mind if the cash they were lending out was their own, rather than belonging to some poor soul who's been convinced to leave it in the bank's care. As far as I'm concerned, the Bible has it right: usury is a sin. What do you think?'

I coughed and turned the conversation to the weather. 'Awful day, always the same at burials.

The forecast on the wireless says we'll have it for the next few days. Warmer by next week, with a bit of luck.'

'Something to look forward to, then. Can I ask you a question?'

'I don't see why not, Alec.'

'You've been looking into Henry's death. Is that right?'

'In a manner of speaking, it is, though "looking into" is a bit stronger than I'd put it. Henry was only missing when Audrey asked me to look for him. I had the bad luck to find his body, that's all. Since then, I've passed on to the police a couple of things I've noticed. I'd rather they did their job properly, but they're dragging their feet. It's part of the reason I've not been able to finish the job you asked me to do. Henry's mother died, so he asked me to hang on for a bit, and now this.'

'Don't worry about my little problem, James, this is much more important. Henry was a good friend to me, and I want his killer brought to justice. If there's anything I can do, anything at all, you let me know and I'll move heaven and earth to make it happen.'

'That's kind of you. As a matter of fact, I'd like to talk to you some more, but this isn't the place. May I meet with you later on?'

'I should be at the factory all afternoon. Give Carol a call and she'll slot you in. If I'm tied up, I shouldn't be too long.' He pointed at the clock. 'Anyway, I must be off. I'll see you later.'

Kendrick zigzagged across the room, talking with the remaining mourners before settling alongside Audrey, and her ever-present sister, for ten minutes before leaving. A blue-rinsed woman in her forties appeared from nowhere and thrust a plate in my direction.

'Sad, sad, time. Poor Audrey. Terrible business, don't you think? Have you eaten, Mr…?'

'Given.' I held my hand up to refuse the plate. 'I've already had plenty, thanks anyway.'

She introduced herself as Mrs Bentley, the vicar's wife, and asked how I knew Henry, so I explained he'd been my superintendent when I was a police inspector. Other questions followed, which I answered politely, though with little detail. Something in the interrogation told me she'd be storing my answers for gossip with her husband later. After a while, she changed tack.

'And you know Mr Kendrick as well?'

'Only a little.'

'Lovely man. He attends Ralph's church. Every Sunday. Ten o'clock service without fail. Always first to make a contribution to any little fundraising efforts we have. Been a churchwarden for a few years now, and exceedingly diligent he is, too. So, so keen on parishioners carrying out good works.'

'In my dealings with him, he's seems decent.'

'Oh, he is. Don't know what we'd do without him.' She glanced theatrically in both directions. 'It's such a shame he's having business worries.'

'The company is struggling, then?'

'Oh, I wouldn't put it as strongly as that, my dear, but a little birdie told me one or two bills haven't been paid.' She dabbed cake crumbs from her lips. 'I'm sure it's nothing. I really shouldn't gossip.'

Without pausing for breath, the vicar's wife hit me with the question she'd really wanted to ask. 'Audrey said you're a detective. Are you hunting for poor Henry's murderer?'

I stepped back and held up my hands. 'That's the police's job. I'm simply a former colleague who had the misfortune to stumble upon his body.' I glanced at my watch. 'I'm afraid I have to go now.'

With this I turned away, leaving her open-mouthed, and told Audrey I needed to leave for a while. She'd offered to put me up for the night, but I'd declined, having booked a cheap bed and breakfast not far away. She'd not need my support, as her sister had arrived, and in my own place, I'd be free to come and go as I pleased.

Outside, Alec Kendrick stood talking to two men who tipped their hats and walked away when he waved me over.

'You can see I've not escaped yet, James. I see the redoubtable Mrs Bentley was giving you the benefit of her wisdom.'

I laughed. 'Interesting lady.'

'I shouldn't speak ill of people, James, but that lady is such a terrible busybody. I suspect she's been telling you all sorts of tales about everyone here.'

'She told one or two, that's the truth.'

'Well, there are always people like that around, and they revel in it at funerals. Such a sad day, and me late. I couldn't get away, so much going on at work.'

'Problems?'

'Quite the contrary. We had a breakthrough today on the aircraft project. One of the men you met, Charlie Bakewell, had a few ideas so I gave him free rein to try them out. One has come up trumps to solve a problem we'd been facing. With luck, we can go into production in a week or two.'

'That will be a relief, then.'

Kendrick looked puzzled. 'In what way?'

'Mrs Bentley said your firm's had a bit of a rough ride recently, so it can't have been easy.'

He folded his arms and puffed out his chest. 'I don't know where she got that idea from at all. Kendrick's is one of the longest established and most well respected firms in the town, and even though the war has brought its challenges, we're still solid enough.'

I apologised and said I must have misunderstood what the woman had been saying.

'Not a problem, James. Easily done with a woman like her.' Kendrick checked his watch. 'I'm sorry, I really must be going. I'm already an hour longer than I said I'd be.'

FIFTEEN

I'd seen a telephone box round the corner from the Dyers' home, so I made my way round there and phoned Bob Moore.

'Hello, James.' The monotone gave away the silent groan when he heard my voice. 'What can I do for you?'

'Can I ask you a favour?'

'You can ask.'

'I've spoken to Phil Trimble, and he says you've always been keen to get the right result.'

'And?'

'There are still things about Henry's death which make me uneasy.'

'Like?'

'Apart from the wallet and all the cash being found, there's the fact that someone was causing petty damage around his home in the weeks before he died. Nothing serious, but enough to show it was malicious.'

'Damage? Where did you hear this?'

'A few weeks ago, Henry told me of a couple of instances. His wife has told me of others which he didn't mention. It seems it may have stopped now he's dead.'

I listed the events, including the incident with the Jack Russell.

'But it's a big jump from a bit of vandalism to killing someone, isn't it?'

'It is, though the poisoning of his dog ramped it up a notch.'

A lorry pulled up beside the telephone box and I had to shield the receiver so the policeman could hear me. 'Also, Audrey told me Henry had met someone from his past recently and it had unsettled him.'

'Interesting. Any idea who?'

I suspected Terry Gleeson, but the time wasn't right to involve the police in chasing someone I could easily find for myself. I also needed to consider other possibilities.

'Audrey didn't know; she just said Henry had mentioned it when she'd asked if he had something on his mind.'

'So what's the favour you want, James?'

'It's in connection with this new information. I'd be grateful if you could find out what you can about Henry Dyer's past. You can access his service record more easily than I can. See if anyone he put away just came out of prison. I know it's a long shot, since he'd been behind a desk for years before he retired, but if he'd arrested someone for a violent crime they might still have been inside until recently. If they were innocent, and held a grudge for all that time, who knows what they'd do?'

The inspector paused. 'I think I can do that. Anything else?'

'Again, it seems unlikely there'll be anything, but perhaps you might ask around at headquarters. Any of his old colleagues ever hear of bad blood? Friends? Family? That kind of thing.'

'I can do that as well, James, but he always seemed so steady to me, not one to ruffle feathers.'

'Well, he ruffled someone's, didn't he?'

'Only if your argument holds water. If I'm right, and it was a random robbery, then we're not going to find the culprit by digging through Dyer's old files and contacts. Still, it's a reasonable line of enquiry. I just wish I had more men to put on it.'

'It's good of you to do what you can, Bob. I know it's difficult at the minute. It must be hell with so many of the young ones leaving to fight.'

'You don't know the half of it. When they asked me to come back, they didn't say we'd be operating with half the lads gone. Those who stayed or were pulled in like me are either past it or useless. We have all the run-of-the-mill villains to deal with, then all the war regulations on top. Last thing I need is a murder on my patch.'

'I don't envy you. It can't be easy. All I can do is thank you for the efforts you're making, especially as you're not convinced I'm right anyway.'

Bob laughed. 'I'm not sure I have much choice, do I, James? You're one of the most persistent blokes I've ever met. Just you remember to keep me up to date, and I'll promise to do the same.'

We hung up, and I called Alec's secretary to arrange a time to meet him.

Carol Wilkins greeted me with a smile and the offer of a cup of tea when I arrived at half past four. I declined the drink, and she went to tell her boss I was waiting. A few minutes later he rang to say he was ready, and she led me through to his office. He closed the door and indicated I should sit.

This was the first time I'd been in his office. On my earlier visits to the factory, we'd met in the foyer, in Carol Wilkins's office and in the room he'd lent to me. It was not as plush as I'd imagined; the desk and cupboards were old, and I guessed they'd been bought in his father's time as head of the company. The carpet was well worn and the whole room looked tired. Its one saving grace was the view of the tree-lined river and a bridge through the windows forming one corner of the room. In the distance beyond those trees, and the green space behind them, lay Henry's house.

'Thanks for hanging on, James. I had something I needed to finish that should have been done this morning. It's out of the way now, and I've an hour to spare if you need it. Shop floor is winding down for the day, so we shouldn't be interrupted.'

'I can't see it taking too long. I just hoped you might have some light to throw on Henry's death.'

'Well, I'll do my best. Bad business there today, so sad.'

'It was. I had a couple of interesting conversations, though. The vicar's wife was telling me of all the good work you do in your church.'

He waved a hand, swatting away the compliment. 'It's nothing. My father always instilled in me that you can't be a Christian without trying to be a good person. Don't you agree?'

I didn't tell him I felt a little unhappy with the implication that it was only Christians who were virtuous. I also didn't mention some of the so-called Christians I'd known who did distinctly bad things like theft, and even murder. I rubbed my thigh at the thought. 'It's very laudable, Alec.' I shifted in my seat. 'So, you're happy to answer some questions?'

'Of course. Ask away.'

'Can you think of anyone who might want to harm him?'

'Henry? Not really. He was the most polite of souls. It's hard to imagine him having a cross word about anything, except perhaps if he was losing at golf.' As Kendrick said this, he frowned and leaned back in his chair.

'Have you remembered something, Alec?'

'You know, now you've asked, something does come to mind. I've been racking my brains ever since I heard his body had been found, trying to imagine who might want to hurt him, and I've got nowhere until just this minute.'

'So who is it?'

'I don't know his name, and it might be nothing at all, but Henry and I were due to meet in the golf club bar a few weeks back. I'd been delayed — something came up here in the factory — and when I got there, Henry was taking some stick from this man.'

'Stick?'

'Well, there are always arguments going on down there: rules, shot selection, best putt, and so on, but this appeared to be more than competitive banter. As far as I could see, Henry kept calm while explaining something, but the other fellow was red in the face and shaking.'

'What happened?'

'Henry just walked away and joined me. I asked him what it was about, and he said it was nothing, just a little difference of opinion.' Kendrick glanced out of the window for a moment. 'I can't say I believed him. Henry was too distracted for it to be so simple, and the man stood at the bar chatting to the steward, even glaring at Henry for a while.'

'And was that it?'

'Not quite. The man finished his drink and left, then, a few seconds later, he pushed through the door again and shook a fist at Henry, shouting that he'd be sorry.'

'You're sure you don't know who he was?'

Kendrick shook his head. 'Can't say I've seen him in there before, though that wouldn't be so odd. A lot of the players only go in the clubhouse to change, so unless we'd played at almost the same time our paths might not cross. I'm certain Henry knew him, though. They hadn't just sparked such an argument there and then.'

'You say this man spoke to the club steward? Do you think he'd have known him?'

'Maybe. It might be worth asking.'

Kendrick told me the steward's name and what time he'd be in the clubhouse. He offered to take me there.

'No thanks, Alec. I'll go and see him after dinner. It's probably better if I'm on my own. Is there anyone else you can think of with a grudge against Henry?'

'No-one. As I said, he was always so even-tempered. Are you sure it wasn't just wrong place wrong time?'

'Possibly, but I'm keeping an open mind.' Alec Kendrick had been a friend of Henry's, a fellow golfer and a drinking partner, so there was no way to avoid my next question. 'Can you tell me where you were the morning he was killed?'

He sat back in his chair, eyebrows knitted. 'You think I had something to do with Henry's death?'

'I have to ask you, Alec. If the police ever get further than the robbery theory, they'll want to talk to everyone who knew Henry and will have the same question. It helps cut down the number of suspects, that's all.'

I thought for a moment that Kendrick wasn't going to answer. Even innocent people feel insulted if their honesty is put under the spotlight, but he scratched his head, then flipped open a leather-bound diary on his desk.

'It still feels a little unpleasant you need to ask, James. I thought we'd become friends. There's a meeting with a client shown in the afternoon, and I'd have been here in the morning, as I usually am during the week. Carol should be able to confirm that, if I need an alibi.'

'There'll be no need for me to check. I'll leave that to Inspector Moore and his colleagues if they find something not adding up. I'm satisfied.'

'That's very decent of you. Now, is there anything else?' He swung a hand over the pile of papers in front of him. 'I've a lot to do, having lost the morning.'

There was little point in asking him anything else. I'd used up all his goodwill for the day, and perhaps a few more days besides. I'd have to do something to make amends, and I hoped I could begin in the next half hour.

On the ground floor of the factory, I watched Alfie Wilson as I had a month earlier. It was exactly the same pattern: most of the men left on time, Bakewell and Carson shortly afterwards, leaving Wilson on his own. He whistled his way across the workshop to the toilets, popped his head around the door, then wandered back and stuffed his briefcase with documents which I assumed contained the latest improvements Alec had mentioned at the funeral.

As the foreman made his way to the door, I nipped outside to make sure I didn't miss him. Outside the factory gate, Alfie Wilson zigzagged through the back streets in a way I couldn't have done as a stranger to this part of the town. I stayed well back, close enough not to lose him but far enough to avoid the foreman recognising me if he glanced round. When he reached The Parade, opposite the very grand Regent Hotel, he turned left, and I had to slow in case he'd stopped round the corner. For a moment I hung around, looking through a butcher's window, then I followed Wilson, confident that if he saw me the delay would convince him it was just a chance encounter in the middle of town.

I needn't have worried. By the time I turned, Wilson was crossing the road a hundred yards ahead and appeared oblivious to anything other than getting home for his evening meal. We walked for another five minutes through streets where the shops and houses steadily became less grand. As yard after yard passed, I hoped my leg would hold out. Finally, he turned into a street of terraced houses, each with a small garden and a low wall in front, and walked up the path of the fifth in the row. I hung around on the corner until he went inside, then I ambled past on the opposite pavement. Most of the properties appeared well maintained, but not Wilson's. Apart from the garden, which was neat and full of bright summer flowers, it was dilapidated and hadn't seen a coat of paint for some years.

I passed by, crossed the road, and knocked on a neighbour's door, one the same colour as Wilson's. A woman I judged to be in her sixties answered, looked me up and down, and raised an eyebrow.

'Yes? Can I help you?'

'Is Alfie home?'

'Alfie? There's no Alfie here.'

I rubbed my chin. 'Works at Kendrick's? Foreman.' I pulled a piece of paper from my jacket pocket and ran a finger across as if checking something. 'Looks like I must have the wrong house. Sorry to have bothered you. They said he lived on this street. They weren't sure of the number, but they said it had a brown door, so I thought this must be the one.'

She stepped forward and pointed further down. 'Would it be Alfie Wilson? He lives four doors down. Theirs is brown. Seem to remember he works there.'

'Ah, that would be it, then. You know him?'

'A little. Nice man, been here a few years. Keeps his garden tidy.' She pulled a face. 'Doesn't do much with the house, though. I expect looking after his wife takes all his spare cash.'

'His wife?'

'Liz. She's in a wheelchair. And her so young.' The woman gave me a sideways look. 'But surely you'd know that, if you're a friend of his.'

'Not really a friend. I know him from work; I'm in the offices there. I had to be over this way tonight and thought I'd pop in and say hello.' I backed away towards the gate. 'Anyway, thanks for your help. I'll get round there now.'

I turned the wrong way out of the gate, on purpose, and she called me back, pointing down the street. 'That way, number thirty-seven.'

Raising my hand in thanks, I waited until she went inside, then hot-footed it to the end of the street, hoping she wasn't peering through her window. I glanced back when I reached the corner. At that moment, Wilson's front door opened and he came out onto the pavement, turning away from me, and strode down the street. In his right hand he had the briefcase.

Despite the throbbing in my thigh I had to follow, praying he'd not walk too far. In fact, it was only round the next corner, and I had to duck back for a few seconds to avoid being seen. If I left it too long I'd miss where he went, so I popped my head round as soon as I thought it safe. Terraced houses lined both sides of a short cul-de-sac, with one row split by a large public house, the Duke of Wellington, its frontage shining with green and maroon tiles in two shades. Wilson disappeared through one of the two entrances.

I gave it a minute before wandering after him and going through the other entrance, into the taproom. The small bar was almost empty and so I ordered a lemonade as quickly as I could, hoping he wouldn't see me and that I could explain my presence away as a coincidence if he did. As I lifted my glass, I spotted Wilson in the other room. I took a seat where I could watch his reflection in a brewery mirror hung over the fireplace. I'd not taken two sips when a man in a brown suit and trilby hat joined him. They spoke for a couple of minutes, Wilson handed over the contents of the briefcase and the stranger passed him an envelope. The man skimmed the papers, grinned, and spoke again, but Wilson shook his head. There was no doubt Wilson was refusing to do what his companion asked.

When I got back to my digs after following Wilson, I ate there, with a diminutive landlady fussing around the guests.

My meal, a stodgy pie with overboiled vegetables followed by a pudding hard to describe, left me full, though not content.

I did what I should have done that morning and telephoned Rachel to say I was sorry. She was distant and uncommunicative, accepting my apology with little grace. I'd been tempted to point out we were both at fault, then decided humility would be the best policy so far from home. We hung up with no movement forward.

Our conversation, the funeral, the meal, and my aching leg left me with no enthusiasm for going to see the golf club steward, though it had to be done.

I lay down for half an hour, but the course was too far out of town to chance walking, even though the rain had cleared and the warm, sunny evening might have made it pleasant. I took a taxi. When I arrived, I asked the driver to collect me again in an hour.

Inside, several tables were occupied by groups of four playing cards. I thought I recognised one of the groups as the men who'd been there when I'd met Henry and Alec, and the way they stared at me suggested the recognition was mutual. I made my way to the bar and ordered a soft drink from the young man serving.

He looked me up and down, and glanced over my shoulder to see if I was with anyone. Clearly my clothes didn't mark me out as either affluent or a golfer.

'You're a member, sir? Or with one?'

'Sorry, I'm neither. Are you Tom Freeman? A friend said I should have a word.'

He confirmed he was and asked what it was about.

'I'm a friend of Henry Dyer. You knew him?'

'Of course. Really sad, what happened to him. Didn't I see you in here with him a couple of weeks back?'

'You probably did. We were with Alec Kendrick. He's the member who gave me your name. Can I ask if you remember Henry having a row with a man in here one night? Sometime in the month before he was killed?'

'As it happens, I do.' He rinsed some glasses and began to dry them. 'Not sure I should be talking about it, though. Member stuff is private.'

'I could say it won't be so private if the police come calling. But we don't want to bother with that, do we?'

I took out my wallet and laid a ten-shilling note on the bar. Freeman looked down, glanced again over my shoulder, then pocketed the cash.

'Bloke called Sebastian Clark, it was. Not been a member long. Terrible at golf, I understand, but we get that sort sometimes.'

'What sort?'

'The ones who only want to make well-heeled contacts. They pay the fees, latch on to other players, and try to sell them something while pretending they're new best mates. Committee tries to keep them out, but now and again one slips through. From what I understand, this Clark is an investment adviser, has a fancy car and, I'm told, a big house down by the Pump Rooms.'

'And you saw them arguing?'

'I was busy out the back, and they'd about finished when I came through. Looked serious, though.'

'Do you know what the argument was about?'

'Naw. All I heard was the raised voices, then that Clark came to the bar, all red in the face and muttering to himself.'

'I was told you were chatting to him.'

'Not me. He finished his glass, I asked if he wanted another and he refused, but that's all that happened between us. Next thing I see, he's back inside, waving a fist and shouting at Mr Dyer. Not been in since. I heard he'd been reported to the committee, so maybe he's been kicked out.'

We were joined at the counter by two men, so I asked Freeman if he had an address for Sebastian Clark. He said he didn't but knew roughly where the house was. He gave me directions and the soft drink I'd asked for.

I sat at a table by the door, drinking my juice, waiting for my taxi, and thinking of the snobbery associated with clubs like this one.

SIXTEEN

Saturday 27th July, 1940

It had been too late to do much else after I'd spoken to Tom Freeman. Even so, I had tried telephoning Alec Kendrick from a box on the corner, but I got no answer. I went back to my lodgings and listened to a play and a variety concert on the wireless. By the time the war commentary came on after the nine o'clock news, my eyes were drooping, and I'd had enough depressing information for one evening, so I toddled off to bed, where I slept like a baby for the first time in a while.

Before going to find Sebastian Clark's house on Saturday morning, I managed to get through to Alec to tell him I'd made some progress on his case.

'Are you going to tell me who it is taking the documents?'

'I need to talk to the men again first. Could you ask them to see me this afternoon? They are working today, aren't they?'

'They are, but they probably won't be impressed.'

'Tell them I'm sorry, but there are a couple of things I need to clarify. If you offer to honour their overtime, it might sweeten the pill. With luck, I'll be able to give you a result afterwards.'

My next call was to Bob Moore, hoping he'd be working at the weekend. My luck was in. 'Any news, Bob?'

'God, you don't give a man much time, do you? Not much has turned up yet, nothing at all in his personal life.'

'Friends? Family?'

'He'd a few friends at the clubs he was in, but they're all social. I can't see any of the chess players or golfers getting annoyed enough to bash an opponent's head in. The wife, Audrey, you know. Henry had no brothers or sisters; he grew up locally and went to school here in Leamington. Comfortably off. I understand his wife came from a family with money. On top, he'd have his superintendent's pension, and I heard his mother left him a good few bob.'

'Ellen Dyer? Would she have had much? I understood she'd been in service before she married Henry's father.'

'I'm afraid I don't know, James. I'm only passing on what I've heard.'

'Perhaps her husband left a nice nest egg, and she never needed it. Anyway, probably no relevance to what we're looking at.'

'I wouldn't think so.'

'So Henry led a perfect life, followed by a perfect retirement?'

'Unless you count getting murdered.'

'There must be something, Bob.'

'Well, nothing in his contacts that I've found. Most of us don't have enemies, you know. I know people I've disagreed with, and some I assume don't like me, but enemies? Not really. How about you?'

He had a point. Only two people I'd ever known had genuinely hated me, and both were now dead. I'd been attacked a few times, almost killed a couple of times, but those were during the course of investigations, nothing personal. 'You said "not much" had turned up,' I said. 'Other than the friends and family, was there something?'

'Only bits and pieces, not enough to spend time on. I've called in a couple of favours and asked some lads at Warwick HQ to keep digging. If they find anything, I'll let you know, but unless you can come up with some credible names soon, James, I'm still putting this down to a robbery gone wrong.'

'Don't bury it just yet. I've two trails to follow. If there's nothing after that, then I might need to concede you're right and leave you to it.'

'Who are they?'

'I'd rather not say at the minute. I'll try to see them both today, and will be in touch if there's anything you need to know.'

I heard Moore take a deep breath. 'Hardly fair, is it, James?'

'What?'

'You've got me running round, poking into all sorts of corners for you, against my better judgment, and you're keeping leads under your hat?'

'They're hardly leads. Especially if you believe Henry's killing wasn't premeditated. Let's say I'm saving your manpower.'

'Very gracious of you.'

'I don't want to fall out over this, Bob. A couple of names have come up, that's all. I'll have a word with the men involved, and will pass them on to you and your boys if it's worthwhile. If not, then you've lost nothing, have you?'

'You make it all sound very reasonable but, believe me, James, if I find you're running an investigation of your own and keeping me out, I'll have you put away. Understand?'

I laughed. 'On what grounds?'

The firmness in Bob Moore's answer told me I'd overstepped the mark. 'How about impersonating a police officer for starters?'

The phone clicked at the other end and I was left on my own.

It was a fifteen-minute walk from the telephone to the Argyll Hotel where I'd seen Terry Gleeson. I rang the bell and an elderly woman in slippers opened the front door. An unlit cigarette dangled from her lip.

'Yes?'

'Is Mr Gleeson home?'

'Him? Gone. Left this morning before breakfast. You a friend of his?'

'In a manner of speaking. Did he say where he was going?'

'No, and I didn't ask. If you see him, tell him he owes me some ration coupons. Told him when he came I needed them. Anything else?'

I asked how long he'd stayed. She refused to answer, saying she couldn't give out private information about her guests. I pulled out my wallet, hoping ten bob might loosen her qualms about keeping her clients' confidences. She closed the door in my face. I'd need to look for Gleeson elsewhere.

The route from the hotel took me through some very rundown streets, past poorly maintained, redbrick terraces. The dirty sash-windows were raised on many of them, allowing the sounds of crying babies, barking dogs and matrimonial arguments to escape into the warm morning. Within a quarter of a mile I came out by the river, to a land as far away from where I'd been minutes earlier as it was possible to imagine.

The houses where Tom Freeman had said Sebastian Clark lived formed a very grand Regency terrace, three storeys high and overlooking a park with bandstand. A discreet brass plate bearing the words "Clark Investments" told me the middle one belonged to the man I was looking for. A thin young woman in domestic uniform opened the door, and I asked if her employer was at home.

'I'm afraid not, sir. He's away for a few days. We expect him back on Tuesday or Wednesday. May I give him a message?'

I asked her for a sheet of paper, and when she returned I wrote a note explaining that Mr Clark didn't know me but I had something I needed to discuss with him, and I'd be grateful if he rang me on his return. The message was vague enough for him to think I might be a potential client, so I was quite sure he'd call. His home didn't look like one acquired by a man who missed an opportunity.

Disappointed at my lack of progress, I called in to say goodbye to Audrey, who now seemed steadier than she'd been at the funeral, even sharing a smile and the offer of a cup of tea, which I refused. I told her there'd been no great progress and that there were still some leads to follow up, but not to raise her expectations. On the doorstep, she squeezed my hand and asked me to do all I could to find Henry's murderer. I could do no more than nod and agree.

An hour later, I sat in the office on the third floor of Alec Kendrick's building with my notepad on my desk and the young engineer, Billy Carson, sitting in front of me.

'I've another couple of questions for you, Billy. Is that all right?'

He shrugged. 'If you must you must, though I can't see what else I can tell you. We went through everything last time, and I'm pretty busy today.'

'I'm sorry about that. It can't be helped. You live with your parents?'

His face slipped into a frown. 'How do you know that?'

I tapped my pad. 'It's all in here. Got it all from your work records. There's not much I don't know about you, Billy. Everything fine at home, is it? No money worries?'

'None to speak of.' The grin came back. 'Could always do with another couple of bob in the pay-packet, if you've any influence with the boss. Dad works here and Mum's got a cleaning job, so we manage. Why?'

Though I was certain Alfie Wilson had been selling details of Kendrick's developments to a competitor, I needed to be sure none of his workmates were taking a backhander as well. I ignored Billy Carson's question.

'Can I ask you if you ever take plans out of the building?'

'No. I told you last time I put them away at the end of the day, or I'd leave them with Mr Wilson if he wanted to work with them.'

'And has he ever asked you to fetch any in particular before you leave?'

'No.'

'You're sure? Ever asked you to drop any round to his house?'

'His house? Why would he do that? If he did, I'd tell him no. It's important work we're doing here, you know. Secret. My brother and most of my friends are in the forces. I'd not do anything to put them in more danger.' The young engineer was shaking and his indignation appeared genuine.

'That's fine, Billy. I just needed to ask. You can go now. Send in Charlie Bakewell, will you?'

He walked to the door and glared back as he twisted the handle. 'I don't know what you're doing here, Mr Given, but it's not what we've been told, I'm sure of that. Next time you want to ask me any questions, let me know in advance and I'll have someone else with me. I'm an honest bloke and won't be treated like I'm not.'

The door was slammed with a little less respect than he'd shown at the beginning of our interview.

I'd been to have a look at the outside of Bakewell's house, as I had at Billy's, after I'd followed Wilson with his briefcase. It was nothing fancy, only what I might have expected of a man in his position — a small terrace in a reasonable part of town, with two children playing outside the front door. There was no car nor any other evidence that Bakewell had a lifestyle beyond the wages Kendrick paid him, but he'd seemed like an intelligent man — clever enough to avoid being obvious about an income on the side.

I asked him about taking designs home and he laughed.

'Why would I do that? No possible use to me outside work. I like my job, but when I leave the factory, that's it. Pays a decent wage and keeps me out of the army, so I'm grateful, but I've no wish to be foreman. Leave that to the likes of Alfie Wilson and Ernie Parkes.'

'Parkes took them home?'

Bakewell blushed. 'Well, I can't say he actually took them home, but he had them at his desk every five minutes. Whenever a new set came out, he'd grab them from the office and scribble away in his little black notebook.'

'Do you know what he was writing?'

'I asked him once, and he gave me such a look I didn't bother again. Anyway, I never take them out unless I have to, and I've never had them out of the factory. So what's all this about?'

'All in good time, Charlie. They're just some questions Mr Kendrick wants me to ask. Do you want to have a word with him? Tell him you're not happy?'

'Didn't say I wasn't happy, did I? Not sure where it's going, that's all.'

'How well do you know your foreman? Go drinking with him sometimes, perhaps?'

'Alfie Wilson? Don't think I've ever seen him take a drink. Not sure he can afford it. Always moaning about the cost of everything when he's at work.'

'You chat a lot at work, do you?'

'Not that much. We might chat now and again over our tea break. About football or what's been on the wireless. That kind of thing. We're not mates.'

I flipped through my notes. 'Can I ask you about your pay, Charlie? Happy with it?'

He shrugged. 'Always room for improvement.'

'I expect so. Two children, haven't you? Can't be cheap with them growing up. Any work on the side to help out?'

'No. What are you suggesting?'

'Nothing, Charlie, nothing. Just asking.' I looked at my notepad again. 'You said last time that you go drinking with some pals once a week. Any of them at factories doing similar work to here?'

Bakewell crossed his arms and leaned back in his chair. 'Listen, I don't understand why you're asking about my mates. What have they to do with anything? We all work in different places, but we don't chat about the job, never have. We meet for a few pints and a laugh, that's all. Can we stick to what I do here, and how we can make it better? That's what you said this was all about.'

'Well, we can stop there anyway, Charlie. I think I've heard enough.'

He went to leave, then turned back. 'You're not going to tell Mr Kendrick what I said, are you, Mr Given? About forgetting work once I've left? I do a good job when I'm here.'

'I'm sure you do. I won't say anything to your boss that isn't relevant to what he's asked me to look at. Please tell Mr Wilson I'll see him now. While you're down there, see if you can find

Mr Parkes's notebook. Bring it up to Mr Kendrick's secretary if you do.'

Bakewell left, with his head hung lower than when he'd arrived, and I waited five minutes for his foreman to join me. I offered him a seat.

'Thanks for coming up, Mr Wilson. I know it's the weekend and you're all very busy, so I won't keep you long. Can I ask you about your wife? It can't be easy.'

'How do you mean?'

'Well, she uses a wheelchair, doesn't she?'

He stiffened. 'How do you know that?'

'Come along, Mr Wilson, it's no secret around the factory, is it?'

'I don't expect it is, but I didn't think anyone would have mentioned it to you.'

'It's amazing what people will tell you if you ask the right questions.' I let my point hang in the air for a few seconds. 'How is she?'

'She has some decent days, but then some not so good, you know. She had a real poorly spell earlier in the year, but now she's improved. We're hoping to go on holiday sometime soon.'

'Must be expensive.'

'The holiday? Not at all. I'll get her on the bus to her brother's in Birmingham, and we'll have a few days there.'

I wondered if the man I'd met on the train the previous month had been Wilson's brother-in-law, so I thought I'd put on a little pressure. It never hurt to pretend you knew more than you did. 'Is that the one who visited you in June? A natty sort of dresser?'

Wilson scratched his head. 'Now, that's not something I've mentioned at work. So how do you know?'

'It doesn't matter how I know. Am I right?'

He nodded. 'Came down on a Friday, just for the weekend. Wanted to see Liz and to invite us over to his place. As I said, it won't cost more than the train fare over there.'

'I wasn't talking about the holiday being expensive, Mr Wilson. The cost of doctors and medicines. Can't be cheap.'

'Oh, that. Well, it isn't easy, but we manage.'

'You remember when I asked you if you ever took plans home from the factory? You denied it.'

'That's because I don't.'

'Then what do you carry in the briefcase?'

Wilson's eyes flickered around the room and he gripped the edge of the chair. 'There's nothing in the case. I bring my sandwiches in it in the morning and take it home empty.'

'Really? Was it sandwiches you gave to the man I saw you with in the Duke of Wellington pub? It didn't look like it from where I was sitting.'

'You followed me?'

'I did. All the way from here to your house, then round the corner. You didn't even wait to have your tea. If you had, I might have left before you went out.'

'Well, you'd no right to be following me. Does Mr Kendrick know about it?'

Unlike Billy Carson's indignation, Wilson's sounded lame. Like a cornered man trying to bluff his way out of trouble.

'Not yet he doesn't, but he will as soon as I call him. He's waiting down the corridor for me to get the truth out of you.'

'You're accusing me of stealing designs from here? For money?' His bravado returned. 'You don't know me, Mr Given, but anyone will tell you I'd never do such a thing. Kendrick's means more to me than almost anything.'

'More than your wife's health? I don't think so.'

'What you saw in the pub was about Liz's health, but I'll not discuss it with you. It's my private business.'

'Then it will be for Mr Kendrick to decide. I don't believe you, but I'm not a policeman, not any longer. He just asked me to look into it for him. I'll phone him now. You'd best sit and think what you're going to say when he gets here.'

Alec Kendrick pushed through the door in less than a minute. I pictured him pacing his office, waiting for me to call.

'Come in and take a seat, Alec. I've finished my investigation and I'll explain what I've found. Then Mr Wilson's got something he wants to tell you.'

I told Alec what I'd seen and heard leading up to the papers being handed over in the Duke of Wellington, and that in my opinion Wilson was the man we'd been looking for. Wilson shot me a look, then rubbed his forehead with his fingers.

'You must know that's not the way it is, Mr Kendrick. Haven't I always been honest?'

Alec nodded and let Wilson tell his story. His wife had fallen down the stairs a year earlier, breaking her back and putting her in hospital for months. Wilson had balanced working all day and visiting her in the evenings. They'd lost her wages and soon their savings were almost gone. One night, a couple of months earlier, he'd felt the need to escape for a drink and, in the pub, he'd met a man who he used to work with. One drink had led to another, Wilson had talked about his job and his money problems, and then the companion had suggested there might be a way out through a friend of his.

'But it's all been so much since Liz's accident. The bills just got bigger and bigger with the doctor and someone to look after her during the day. In the end, I couldn't refuse. It seemed the only option.'

Kendrick glanced at me before leaning towards Wilson. 'So you did take money?'

'What? Well, yes, but not for those drawings. It was for my insurance policies.'

'Policies?' Alec frowned. 'Surely they would cost you money?'

'They have. Twenty years, I've been paying. Only a few bob a week, but it mounts up. The chap Mr Given saw me with in the pub gives loans against them. A friend told me about him and it seemed one way out of the mess Liz and me are in. He hangs on to the paperwork, we keep up the premiums, and when one of us dies he gets paid back. Liz didn't want us to do it, but I got a really big bill this week and had no option.'

Kendrick listened without speaking while Wilson poured it all out. He looked at me. 'Don't you think that explains it, James?'

'Could you and I have a couple of minutes alone?'

He agreed and we went to his office. There was no need to lock the door on Wilson; he had nowhere to go without leaving his sick wife.

'I'm sorry, Alec, but you need to be careful. It's a plausible story, but I've heard hundreds in my time. The man has debts, knows the value of those designs, and has ample opportunity to take them away. I even saw him hand them over.'

'You saw him hand something over, James. You believe it to have been my plans, but Alfie says they were insurance policies.'

'Then you do what you wish. I know it's all circumstantial. If I had time I'd keep digging and tidy it up, but I can't spare any more. Henry's murder must take precedence. I've been wrong before, though I don't think I am on this one.'

Kendrick took a deep breath, clapped his hands, and stood. 'I hear what you're saying, James, and I thank you for all you've done. Now, let's get back in there.'

When we sat facing Wilson again, Kendrick leant across the desk and laid his hand on the man's forearm.

'Why didn't you tell me you were having problems, Alfie? Perhaps I could have helped.'

'I don't know, sir. I should have trusted you to see me right.'

'I'd have done what I could. Now you've put me in a very difficult position. I want to believe what you've told me, but Mr Given says the facts point to you having stolen from me.'

Wilson dropped his head into his hands. 'Are you going to call the police?'

Kendrick didn't answer straight away. He rubbed his chin and stared at the foreman engineer.

Wilson was now shaking, his eyes filled with fear. 'Please don't, sir. I didn't do anything wrong, but if I go to prison, what will become of my Liz?'

His boss's next words surprised me. 'No, Alfie. I don't think I'll call in the police, though I can't decide if you're telling me the truth.'

'Thank you, sir.'

For the first time, the foreman relaxed in his chair, the relief obvious on his face until Kendrick spoke again.

'Of course, I'll have to take your present position from you and promote one of the men.'

It hardly seemed possible for Wilson to slump any lower, but he did. There were tears in his eyes when he looked up. 'But Mr Kendrick, sir, I can't afford to take a cut in wages. I'll be even worse off than I was before. You're good to trust me like this, and I shouldn't complain. I'll put in as many extra hours as I can manage if you'll let me stay as foreman.'

Kendrick didn't pause for a second. 'I'm sorry, Alfie, but I don't think you understand. It's the principle. You may have betrayed my trust and put an important contract in jeopardy. If we'd lost it because a competitor stole our methods and undercut us, then I might have had to lay men off. How would their families manage then?'

Wilson opened his mouth to protest, but Kendrick cut him off.

'If I put you on piecework like most of the other men, with your skill you'll easily earn almost as much as you do now, and I'll make sure you get as much overtime as you need. I'll tell everyone you've been finding the pressure of the foreman's job a bit much with all that's going on at home, so we've agreed for you go back to general production. That should stop any tongues wagging.'

Alfie Wilson left a few minutes later, after his boss had asked to see him again in a couple of days, when they'd talk about how he might help financially. When he'd gone, Kendrick rubbed his eyes and sighed.

'That was awful, James. Have I made the right decision?'

'I think you've been more than generous. You'd have been well within your rights to turn him over to the police and make an example of him.'

'But what would that have achieved, especially if he wasn't guilty? I'd have lost an excellent worker, and Alfie would probably have gone to jail, making the situation with his wife impossible for the pair of them. This way, if he did do it, I'm convinced he'll go and sin no more, as the Good Book says.'

'Then all I can repeat is that you're being more generous than many would have been.'

'I have to do what I believe to be right. Speaking of which, how much do I owe you for your time?'

I told him he owed me nothing, that our dead friend had asked for a favour, and I owed him more than one.

'Well, the least I can do is cover your expenses, James, and offer you accommodation in my home any time you fancy a trip to Leamington.'

I took him up on his offer to reimburse my train fares, and said I'd perhaps accept the opportunity for a weekend away at some point. He left, and a few minutes later Carol brought me a cheque for my expenses.

'I've ordered a taxi for you, Mr Given, but Charlie Bakewell came up with a message for you. He said he'd searched and couldn't find Mr Parkes's notebook. Do you need to stay and talk to Charlie again?'

I told her I didn't. As I waited for the cab I smiled, pleased I'd been able to help Alec Kendrick. However, I wondered if my conclusions had been right, and how someone with such a forgiving nature could succeed in business.

On the way, I collected my things from my lodgings, then took a train to Coventry, dreading the reception I'd get from Rachel for making the diversion.

'Hello, Terry.'

Gleeson's jaw dropped when he answered the rap on his door to find me on his front step. I'd thought it worth taking a chance that he still lived at the same address in Coventry when we'd worked together. The detour by train was minor, and his home was only a ten-minute walk from the railway station, through leafy streets and past well-tended gardens. The houses, though not in the same league as Sebastian Clark's, or even the Dyers', spoke of a level of affluence above that of the ordinary factory or shop worker. Here lived many of the managers and engineers who kept the city's car industry in fine fettle and whose wages reflected their importance.

Gleeson, in pyjamas and unshaven, despite it being almost teatime, looked out of place. As a police inspector he'd not have been badly paid, but I had no doubt the corrupt backhanders had helped him afford such a nice neighbourhood.

'What the hell are you doing here, Given?'

'That's not nice, is it, Terry? Aren't you going to invite me in?'

'Not if you're poking your nose in my business again.'

I shrugged. 'That's fine, then. I'll get back to Birmingham and let the Leamington police handle it. I should have just passed your name on in the first place, saved myself a trip.'

To say Gleeson and I had history would have been an understatement, and his dislike of me might ordinarily have resulted in the door being slammed in my face, but my mention of the police made him think. His shoulders dropped and he swung the door wider.

'There's no need for that. You'd better come in.'

He led me down the hall to a sitting room which hadn't been tidied in a good while. Gleeson swiped a cat off an armchair and offered me its place. The stained fabric and mat of hairs made me think twice, but there seemed no alternative, and I needed to rest my leg.

'So, what do you want to know, Given?'

'Only what I asked you last time. Why were you in Leamington?'

He sneered. 'I fancied a few days away.'

'Really? In that dump of a "hotel"? Hardly a weekend at The Ritz, was it?'

'Huh. Perhaps not.'

'I think you were there to see Henry Dyer. His wife said he'd recently met someone from his past.'

'What if I did? That's not a crime.'

'No, but murder is.'

Gleeson slammed his hand down on the arm of his chair. 'Murder? You know, I thought that's why you were chasing me. Well, you're wrong. I didn't murder Dyer. Why would I?'

'A mutual friend told me he'd stopped your pension. A court might think that would be enough. Especially if the jury knew you'd killed before.'

'You've no evidence I ever killed anyone, Given. If you did, you'd have had me inside ages ago. Even if I had, I'd not be so stupid as to kill a copper, even a retired one.'

'But you did see him. Why?'

'To try to convince him to get my money reinstated.' He swung his open palm around the room. 'Look at this place. My wife's left me and my savings are almost gone. If I don't get that pension back, I'll have to sell the house.'

It wouldn't have been helpful to tell him my heart bled. 'And how did that go?'

'I'd telephoned him a few times asking him to change his mind, and Dyer told me to forget it. Said he'd thought about it for a long time before arriving at his decision. The last time I rang, he accused me of trying to intimidate him.'

'You were the one who vandalised his property and tried to kill his dog?'

Gleeson stood and paced the room. 'What are you talking about, Given? I'm not proud of some of the things I've done, but I only wanted Dyer to sort out my pension. I never vandalised his place. Nor hurt his damned dog.'

I shook my head. 'I don't believe you. I think all of this escalated when you met Henry in the park that Monday morning. He turned you down, so you smashed him over the head and left him to die in the bushes.'

'No. No, I didn't. I followed him on the Saturday before his death and cornered him about to go into a café. He said he couldn't talk, he had an appointment, but he'd hear me out later. We agreed to meet on a bench just inside the park gates by the bridge. We met, and I didn't see him again after that.'

'And how did it go? Reject you again, did he?'

'Actually, he listened to me get it all off my chest and, when I'd finished, the boss said he'd think about putting a word in for me.'

'Where were you the morning he was killed?'

'I was here. I came home after I'd spoken to Dyer on Saturday morning and didn't go back over to Leamington until Monday lunchtime.'

'Can anybody confirm that?'

He glared at me but didn't answer.

'So why did you go back?'

'Dyer had had a couple of days to think about what I'd said, so I decided to check if he'd done anything about it. I went round to his house and there was a copper knocking on the door, so I left it. I stayed over to catch him the next day, then you told me he'd been killed.'

'This all seems very convenient — nothing I can check on, is there? No witness to you being at home at the relevant time. And no Henry to disagree with your version of events. Come on, Terry, where were you on Monday morning, really?'

'I don't have to answer any of this, you know, Given. You're not a copper anymore. But for your information, I had a

154

doctor's appointment at ten o'clock. Should be easy enough for you to check if you want. Now, are we finished?'

'Gleeson, you're a fool. If this is true, and believe me, I *will* check, you could have saved us both a lot of bother by telling me about the appointment when I first asked.'

Terry Gleeson had been a police officer long enough to know better than to provide an alibi which wouldn't stand up. Just to make sure, I got the details of his doctor, then left him to it.

SEVENTEEN

Saturday 27th July, 1940

When I called him from Birmingham, Bob Moore took some convincing to agree to make contact with Gleeson's doctor. He didn't think the pension would be enough of a motive, not for an ex-copper. So I had to fill him in on all of Gleeson's past wrongdoing, including why he'd been forced to leave rather than facing a long stretch inside, or even dangling at the end of a rope.

'That all sounds pretty scary, James, but you said Henry Dyer had agreed to think about withdrawing his objections to Gleeson's pension.'

'I didn't say it, Gleeson did, and we only have his word for it. I wouldn't trust him as far as I could throw him.'

'What about the alibi?'

'Admittedly I don't think he's stupid enough to tell such an obvious lie, but come on, Bob, how many fake alibis have you heard in your time? Some criminals think we'll just believe them and not check.'

I heard him laugh. 'I'm sure you're right, though you'd hope an ex-copper would have more sense.'

Moore went quiet and I left him to think. I only had to wait a moment.

'All right, James, I'll check the alibi and see if I can find anything else on him.'

I was about to thank him and let him get on with his day when he hit me with an offer I hadn't anticipated.

'You know they're still looking for senior men, James?'

'Who?'

'The force. I've asked my boss, and he'd sign you up as an inspector in the Specials.'

'But I left because of injury.'

'He said it wouldn't matter; we're desperate with so many of the younger blokes volunteering for the army. He's spoken to some of the lads at HQ, and there's no-one round here with your murder experience. He said he'd assign a sergeant to help if you'd come on board, even just to find Henry Dyer's killer.'

'Why couldn't he do that without me signing my name on the line?'

'He just said it's got to be done officially. What do you think?'

What I thought was that Rachel would have my guts for garters. But it did have its attractions. I'd be free of my father for a while at least, and I'd have the time to spend on Henry's case. With luck, it would be wrapped up in a week or two. Then I could pack it in and get back to normal.

'It's an interesting offer, Bob, but I'll need to discuss it with my wife. Can I get back to you?'

'No problem. Give me a call when you've made a decision. But don't leave it too long. I can't continue committing time to investigating Henry's death unless I have you as extra manpower. And before you say you're already putting the time in, I've said you need to be official, not a lone wolf.'

Rachel was in the kitchen when I finished on the telephone, scrubbing pans which didn't need scrubbing. She'd hardly acknowledged me since I'd arrived home, making it clear she was still fuming about my absence. I stood in the doorway, silently watching her and imagining what my life would be like if she was no longer in it. She'd knocked me off my feet when we'd first met, though her attraction had been much, much more than her stunning good looks. In an instant, she'd known how to reach under my stuffy exterior. In the good times and the dark times over the last year or so, we'd grown closer and closer.

Rachel turned and must have noticed the look on my face at the thought of losing her.

'What is it, James? Bad news?'

I shook the frown away. 'News, but I'm not sure if it's bad.'

I didn't want to tell her what Bob Moore had said without putting it in context. A lot had happened since we'd argued on Thursday night, and I needed to explain why I might even be considering his offer. I asked if she'd sit and listen for a few minutes. She dried her hands, pulled out a chair from under the table, and sat with her arms wrapped tightly round her middle.

I took the other chair and went through everything I'd discovered between finding Henry's body and his funeral, then moved on to the events of the last couple of days.

'So you think Terry Gleeson's got something to do with Henry's death?'

'He has an alibi, so I'm beginning to doubt it. Bob Moore has said he'll check it out.'

'If it's right, what will happen then?'

'There's the problem. He's stretched to breaking point with the men he's got and said he can't do much more without me.'

'Without you?'

As we talked, Rachel's voice softened, and I thought she was starting to see things from my perspective. It didn't last. When I told her what Moore had suggested, the arms were pulled in tighter and the frost returned.

'So what did you say to him?'

'That I'd talk to you.'

'What's it got to do with me? You'll do what you want, James, you always do.'

'That's not true, and you know it.'

'I'm not sure I do. I've told you that I don't want you getting involved in anything where you might get hurt, but you ignore me. We went to France for a quieter life, and you were up to your ears in a murder within five minutes. We come back here and you're investigating a theft and Henry's death, and now you're thinking of rejoining the police, at a time like this. Just so you can put yourself at risk with another madman.'

'Then tell me what I should do, Rachel? Do I walk away? Bob Moore has already said they don't have men who've worked murder cases. At least this way I'll have the authority to investigate properly and have some official help. Would you rather Henry's killing went unsolved?'

She unfolded her arms and leant forward. 'If it means *you* don't get killed, then yes, I would.' Tears began to roll down her cheeks. 'You're getting in far too deep, James, and I'm afraid I'll lose you this time. If that's the way it's going to be, then I can't stop you, but I'm not happy. You'll have to go if it becomes too much.'

'Go how?'

'I can't have you living here, with me scared all the time that there'll be a knock on the door and a sympathetic-looking policeman standing on the step. If it looks like you're in danger, we're finished.'

'But —'

'I'm sorry, James. That's the way it's got to be. Now, leave me to my housework and you telephone your father. He's almost as angry with you as I am and wants an apology.'

I stayed at the table for a minute and watched her walk back to the sink, where her shoulders shook, though she didn't make a sound. When I could face it no longer, I went through to the living room and called my father. It was past sunset and Sabbath was over, so at least I wouldn't be adding to the sins he thought I should atone for.

He was distant, in that quiet way parents have when their children disappoint them, when the conflict between love and anger is at its most tense. Monosyllables came back when I asked about Mama and Sarah, my sister, and I was on the verge of hanging up when he put his first question.

'Are you coming back to work on Monday, Jacob?' I said I was. 'And that will be the last time you leave me in the lurch?'

I couldn't lie to him. 'I'll have to see.'

After I'd said goodnight to him, I leaned back in my armchair and rubbed my eyes. The past few days had taken their toll, and I couldn't face any further disagreements with my father or Rachel.

I spent the rest of the evening on my own, going through my notepad. Rachel practised her scales until, at nine, I took her a cup of Horlicks. She stopped playing, tersely said "thank you", then returned to the piano. Back in my armchair, I switched on the wireless and listened to the reports of a couple of dozen air raids the previous night. There were few casualties, but I wondered how long it would be before Birmingham took a turn.

On Monday evening, soon after I arrived home from work, I was cutting the lawn when I heard the telephone ring through the open window. Rachel came to the back door and gave me her longest sentence since Saturday night.

'It's Inspector Moore. He says he has some information.' She stepped outside and walked to her vegetable bed. 'I'll be out here in the garden if you want me.'

I went inside, took a seat and rubbed my forehead as I lifted the receiver. 'Evening, Bob. You've found something?'

'Well, not really. That your wife? She sounds nice.'

'Rachel? She is. Most of the time. What is it?'

'I had one of my lads contact Terry Gleeson's doctor today. He confirmed your man was with him when he said he was.'

'No mistake? Not earlier or later?'

'None..'

'So he's in the clear. I thought he'd be too cute to give a false alibi. Anything else?'

'Not so far. Have you thought about what I said the other day?'

'I have, but I honestly don't know. Rachel's not keen, and that's putting it mildly. I'll let you know in a day or two.'

We'd barely said goodnight when the telephone rang again. This time, Alec Kendrick was on the other end.

'Any news on Henry's murder, James?'

I told him the suspect I'd had was no longer in the frame.

'Have you managed to track down the fellow Henry argued with in the golf club?'

'Your steward, Tom Freeman, gave me a name, but when I went to the man's house he was away until tomorrow. He's apparently some kind of investment adviser. I'll try to contact him again if you can find me a number in your local directory.'

The line went quiet for a few moments after I gave him Sebastian Clark's name. There was the sound of pages turning, then he returned with the details.

'Only one in the book, James. I don't recognise his name, but I know the address. Nice. Very nice. Must be good at this investment lark. You be careful if you meet him, though. He looked a nasty piece of work when he confronted Henry.'

'I think I'll be fine, Alec. You're sure you don't know him?'

'I don't believe I'd seen him before that night in the clubhouse. He looked like he'd some temper on him, though. Fuming when he went out.'

'Well, I'll be careful and I'll let you know if I find out anything. If you get the chance, ask some other members if they know Clark, and what connection he had with Henry.'

EIGHTEEN

Tuesday 30th July, 1940

I was halfway through breakfast when the door knocker rattled. A policeman stood on the step when I opened up.

'Mr Given, is it, sir?'

I nodded and he handed me an envelope bearing my name, care of my local police station.

'This was sent over from Warwick HQ, sir. My sergeant asked if I'd bring it to you. Will there be a reply?'

I ripped it open and scanned the note inside. 'Not just now, constable. Thanks for taking the trouble.'

He tapped the brim of his hat and wished me a good morning.

Indoors, I read the note again. A Sergeant Baines, who I'd bumped into once or twice, had looked through Henry's old case files and come across two possible leads. The first, a man named Derek Taylor, had been jailed for killing a workmate in a drunken fight and had always claimed it was self-defence. Henry, then an inspector, had been the investigating officer and found there'd been bad blood between the man and his victim, who'd had an affair with Taylor's wife. This had been the deciding factor at his trial, and he was lucky to have been handed down a life sentence, rather than the death penalty. As he'd been taken from the court, Taylor had yelled threats at Henry, saying he'd kill him and all his family if he ever got out.

Baines had discovered that Taylor had been released from prison in the autumn of the previous year.

The second part of the sergeant's report referred to a case Henry had worked on a year or two before I'd joined the force. He'd moved up a rank by that time and oversaw the investigation of the loss of a large sum of money from a company where a woman, Christine Grainger, was working as assistant to the chief accountant. The accountant had reported it to the police, but the next day the offices had burnt down, destroying many of the records. The chief accountant's body was found in the ruins, and the position of the body indicated he'd been trying to escape. Fire investigations revealed it was arson, with a strong indication that the chairs in the reception area had been doused with petrol. Henry had argued it must have been someone senior with access to the building after hours.

Checks on the accountant's finances showed no irregularities, and so suspicion turned elsewhere. Due to the amount of money involved, and pressure from the company owner on Henry's bosses, Henry put men on investigating those with access to the company's cash. Christine Grainger was discovered to be enjoying an expensive lifestyle, though her joint income with her husband, Stephen, was modest. She was pulled in and questioned, and though her husband vouched for her alibi, Dyer decided to push it to trial. She was found guilty and sentenced to twenty years, and had recently died in prison. Grainger's husband continued to fight the case through the courts, always protesting her innocence.

I didn't know if Bob Moore had been sent a copy of the note, or if Sergeant Baines had simply passed the information to me, so I rang Bob at Leamington. He said he'd not seen anything, and I heard him scribbling on a pad. If I'd been in his shoes, I'd have wanted a word with Baines, asking why he'd sent information relevant to an ongoing investigation to a civilian, rather than a superior officer in charge of the case.

Bob continued to make notes as I went through the new material with him, then sighed when I finished.

'So what now, James?'

I chanced my arm. 'If you can get hold of addresses for Derek Taylor and for Christine Grainger's husband, I could interview them both and report back.'

'You're taking up the offer of the job, then?'

I laughed. 'Not yet.'

'James?'

'I'm sorry, Bob. The time's not right, but I'll tell you what I'll do. If I talk to these two and we think there's mileage in looking further, then I'll let you have a proper decision. Fair enough?'

'I expect it will have to be. But don't mess me about. Give me a few days and I'll see what we can find.'

Sebastian Clark's maid had said he'd be home on Tuesday, and I was about to telephone him after dinner when he called me. A refined voice, deep and syrupy. A million miles from the aggressive person Alec Kendrick had described.

'Good evening, Mr ... Given? You left a message to call. How can I help you?'

I thanked him for phoning back and asked if he'd be willing to meet.

'It would be a pleasure, but could you give me an idea what it is about? Then I can think about possible investments in advance.' That voice was designed to assure me my money would be safe with him, even before we'd discussed any business.

'I'm afraid it's not about an investment, Mr Clark. I'd rather not go into too much detail on the telephone, but it's to do with the death of Henry Dyer.'

A pause, then a new edge to his words. 'I know nothing about that.'

'But you knew him?'

'Only slightly.'

'Then I need to talk to you.'

'Are you police, Mr Given?'

'No, I'm not, but I can ask them to talk to you instead, if that's easier for you.'

Once again I'd needed to make a threat rather than showing a badge of authority. If this investigation continued much longer, I'd seriously need to consider accepting Bob Moore's proposal that I should join the Special Constabulary, even for a short time.

'There'll be no need to bring them into it. Can you see me tomorrow?'

'Not until early evening. I can catch a train from Birmingham a little after four and be with you around five. Would that be acceptable?'

Once we'd agreed, I called Alec Kendrick to tell him I'd set up the meeting.

The mantel clock struck ten, and I'd switched off the wireless ready to follow Rachel to bed when someone tapped on the front door. I could barely make out Terry Gleeson's face when I answered, and I was only sure it was him when he spoke.

'I need to talk, Given.'

'What are you doing here at this time of night? Can't it wait until morning?'

'Seriously, this is important.'

Already the dim lamp in the hall was casting enough light onto the street to get me in trouble about maintaining blackout. I glanced up and down the pavement, but there was no warden in sight.

'You'd best come in.' I led him through to the living room but didn't offer him a seat. 'What is it?'

'I wanted to clear the air. We got off on the wrong foot.'

'And whose fault is that?'

'A bit of both, I expect. Will you hear me out?'

The man had killed someone, though it was a man I might have killed myself if I'd thought I could get away with it. He'd been corrupt as a policeman and he'd insulted me enough times for it still to rankle. I wasn't sure why I should listen to him, but I took an armchair.

'You'd better sit down and get on with it. But make it quick. I don't want to be here all night.'

'I'll need to go back a bit to make sense of what I want to say. Is that all right?'

'Just get on with it.'

'Fine. When I left the force, I hit the bottle. Even though I'd not been a great copper —'

'That's putting it mildly.'

'Even though I'd never been a great copper, not dedicated like you, the job was all I'd ever done. I thought I'd have a soft life afterwards, but it didn't turn out that way. I'd had it cushy, and when it was taken away from me I went downhill. Drink, arguments, stomping around feeling sorry for myself. It didn't take too long for my wife to leave me. With Linda gone, it just got worse. Down the pub whenever it was open, then home with the whisky. Not eating and spending my days shouting at the walls. Then for some reason I woke up one morning with a clear head and saw what a mess I'd made of things.'

Despite what I thought of Gleeson, I had a good idea what he was talking about. Drink can take a man to unimaginable depths, and while the booze keeps going down the neck it's impossible to climb out. For the last year I'd kept on top of it most of the time, but even when I'd fallen, Rachel had been there to help pull me up again. If Linda Gleeson didn't have that strength, she wasn't to be blamed. It could be a hard sentence, living with a drunk.

I asked if he wanted a cup of tea. Before he answered, Rachel swung open the door and popped her head round. She looked at me, then Gleeson, then back again.

'Oh. You have a visitor.'

I introduced him and he stood to shake her hand.

'Evening, Mrs Given. I'm sorry to call so late. I … I needed to speak with your husband, but I'll go. We can do it another time.'

'No, Mr Gleeson, please don't leave on my account. I heard voices, that's all, and wondered who it was. I'm off back to bed.' Rachel glanced at me again, her eyes widening as she did. 'James can join me when he's ready.'

She nodded to us both and closed the door. I made us both a hot drink, then returned to the living room. Gleeson looked around before he spoke.

'Nice place you have here. Nice wife, too. You're a lucky man.'

'Most of the time I think so. Are you going to tell me why you're here?'

'I wanted to tell you I had nothing to do with Henry Dyer's murder. I know you don't want to believe me, but it's true. When I met him in Leamington on the Saturday before he was killed, it was just as I told you. We talked, I explained about where I'd got to in my life, I confessed everything I'd done, and I apologised. With him no longer a copper, or my boss, I thought I could chance admitting the lot. At first he said he felt like calling in some old friends still on the force and having me arrested. When I said he had every right to do so, he asked me why I'd done the things I'd done. As we went through them, one after the other, I could see him slowly changing his mind until, at the end, he said he accepted I was sorry. We parted on quite good terms, with him promising he'd have a serious think about the pension situation. I left, truly believing he'd put in a good word.'

I sat quietly for a minute, taking in what he'd said. I already knew his alibi was solid, so he couldn't have killed Henry. I told him. Gleeson slumped back in his seat and puffed out his cheeks.

'That's a relief. Now I need to make another apology. To you.'

'To me? Huh. I think you owe me more than one.'

'All right. I agree. Don't make it more difficult than it already is. I'm not going to bother with everything that went on between us when we worked together. I made some bad choices then, and you're not going to forgive me for some of the things I said anyway. I wanted to say I'm sorry for the way I reacted in the last couple of weeks. You jumped me in that café and I didn't have time to think it through. Then when you came to my house, I felt cornered.'

'That's all very nice, Terry, but where's this going? There was no need to come over here this late. You could have put it all in a letter.'

He tutted. 'What I'm trying to say is that Henry Dyer was always decent to me, even at the end. I understand he hadn't had much choice in contesting my pension. I even heard he was the one who suggested I got it in the first place.'

'He was.'

'There you are, then. I believed him when he said he'd reconsider, and I want to help find who killed him. Not least because it will prove I didn't.'

Gleeson's offer rocked me. We'd never got on. I'd even punched him once. But he sounded sincere. He may have been a corrupt copper, willing to take the easy route and an easy pay-out, but he'd been a detective and collared plenty of villains who hadn't bothered to try a bribe. I gave it a minute and decided he was worth a chance.

'If you're being straight, and God help you if you're not, then I could use an extra head on this. Have you time to go through it now?'

'My last train is in half an hour, so I can't stay just now. Sorry.'

'Well, I've got to travel back to Leamington tomorrow evening. Should I go via Coventry?'

NINETEEN

The ten past four out of Birmingham pulled away almost empty, too early for the workers and shoppers heading home, and too late for day-trippers heading south. My compartment was warm and stuffy, and even pulling down the window provided no relief. Thankfully, the journey to Coventry took no time and I was out on the platform with Terry Gleeson in half an hour.

He said he knew a pub around the corner which would be open, so we walked there in silence. Gleeson and I had spent so many hostile years we weren't about to start chatting like best friends overnight. When we arrived, the place was closed, but Gleeson rapped on a side door and a giant of a man answered.

'Terry, what do you want? We're shut.'

'Let us in, Jimmy. We don't want a drink, just a seat until you open, then we'll be away.'

Jimmy shook his head, then swung open the door, waving a hand to invite us in. 'Go in the snug, you won't be no bother in there.' The way he spoke suggested he'd let Gleeson into the pub outside of hours more than once.

We went through to a room around fifteen foot square, with wooden-topped cast-iron tables, leather-covered bench seats and a stained carpet. It stank of last night's stale beer and cigarettes, enough to put anyone off either. Gleeson indicated one of the seats away from the frosted window.

171

'This will do; no-one will disturb us. Do you want a drink? Jimmy looks a bit intimidating, but he'll get you one if you want.'

I said I wouldn't bother. 'I thought you'd stopped?'

'I have. More or less. Still take the odd pint, but off the hard stuff. Won't bother today.'

'I'm not sure I could manage that kind of control. It's all or nothing for me. Shall we have a look at what I've gathered so far?'

'That's what I'm here for.'

I pulled out my notes and ran through the investigation so far. Gleeson bristled when I covered the section about my suspicion of him, then he grinned.

'You can cross that bit out now, I expect. What else do you have? I assume you've thought about friends and colleagues?'

'Naturally. Dyer had no immediate family. Both parents dead, no brothers or sisters.'

'The wife? Audrey, isn't it?'

'Hardly. She was the one called me to look for him when he didn't come home. Aside from that, Henry was a big bloke and she's small and slim. She'd never overpower him, nor have the strength to bash him so hard as to kill him.'

'Anyone whose nose he put out of joint?'

'Henry played golf, chess and bowls — hardly pastimes where he'd make enemies, are they? Not much of a pub drinker, I'm told — he went to the golf club regularly, and I've met his drinking pal from there. He put me on to this man I'm seeing after I leave here, Sebastian Clark. Seems they had some kind of argument a few weeks ago.'

Gleeson asked if I'd managed to find anyone who'd been arrested by Henry and might still hold a grudge.

'There are two whose names I've been sent. Derek Taylor, who killed someone in a fight and claimed it was self-defence, and Christine Grainger, done for embezzlement and manslaughter, who always pleaded innocence.'

'Worth following up.'

'Actually, she's dead. She died in prison, so it couldn't have been her. Might be the husband; he fought her case all the way.'

'So what are the next steps?'

'Well, I'm off to Leamington to interview Clark, and I've asked for the addresses of Taylor and Stephen Grainger. When I get them, I'll go and have a chat.'

Gleeson and I threw ideas around for another few minutes, but came up with nothing more. We agreed he'd continue to think about possibilities and let me know if anything occurred to him. I also asked if he'd try to trace the addresses I needed. It wouldn't hurt to add to Bob Moore's efforts.

At half past five, the landlord opened the doors, and the pub began to fill with early drinkers. I left Gleeson in their company and walked back to the station to catch my connection.

The second train was no fresher than the first, made worse by it being fuller, so I stood in the corridor near a window, and looked out across the fields of wheat almost ready to harvest. I was glad to step out to the marginally cooler air on the platform when we rolled to a stop.

The streets of Leamington Spa were wide along my route, with grand houses and tree-lined open spaces on both sides of the river providing welcome shade. Clerks and shop-girls were beginning to make their ways home, and small groups gathered at bus stops along the way. Soon after I crossed the bridge, I turned into a side street, quieter and narrower than the others, and only a few minutes' walk from my destination. Twenty steps ahead of me, two men stopped and began an argument. The smaller of them swung a punch, narrowly missing the chin of the larger, who grabbed his arm then dragged him down an alleyway between two houses.

I quickened my step, then heard cries for help. One of the men was getting the worst of the exchange. Looking around, I could see no-one else in earshot, so I had to dive in to help on my own. I had my walking stick, and hoped I and the man taking the beating might overpower the other between us. Sounds of scuffling came from a yard beyond a gate on my right. I pushed it open, only to be dragged in and slammed face-first against a wall.

I was relieved of my stick and held with one arm behind my back. When I was swung round, the big man faced me. I didn't recognise him.

'Think you're clever, don't you, Mr Given?'

I struggled, but the grip only tightened. 'Do I know you?'

'I doubt it. But you do know a friend of ours, and he'd rather you stopped asking questions. Alright?'

'Who's the friend?'

A bone-crunching slap almost took my head off. 'That's the sort of question you shouldn't be asking.'

I spat blood on the ground and tried to focus. 'If I don't know who it is, how do I know what to avoid?'

His fist smashed round the side and into my kidney. My knees buckled, and the big man bent and pressed his nose against mine.

'Perhaps you shouldn't be asking about anyone, then.'

I remembered nothing else until I woke face-down in the dusk, a large ginger cat licking my cheek. My head and torso screamed when I tried to lift myself from the ground. I gave up for a minute, then took a deep breath and steeled myself for another effort. From one knee I managed to reach the wall and claw my way to a standing position. My stick lay where I'd had it wrenched from my grip, and I endured another bout of pain to pick it up, then hobbled back out to the street.

There was no-one about to help, so I leant on a house wall until a car rounded the corner, then launched myself towards it, arms flailing. The eyes of the driver widened as he swerved to avoid me, before revving away down the street. Spent with the effort and feeling like I wanted to be sick, I dragged myself to the corner where the car had come from. I offered a sincere prayer when a cab stopped after a couple of minutes. The driver offered to take me to hospital, but I told him to drop me at the railway station. I needed to go home.

Rachel was less accepting of my wishes than the cabbie. She insisted we go to casualty, where doctors poked and prodded, each of them telling me I was lucky, and it could have been worse. With my ribs strapped I didn't feel lucky, but they released me after an hour with codeine tablets, saying it would hurt for a week or two, and to rest as much as possible.

We returned home, where Rachel put me to bed. I didn't sleep much with the pain, and with the sound of her tears in the darkness. It gave me plenty of time to think about who had set the thugs on me. Whoever it was clearly wanted me to lay off my investigation, so they must have thought I was getting close. My discussion with Terry Gleeson had shown I wasn't. I'd no clearer idea of a feasible suspect than when I'd started, particularly with Gleeson himself now out of the frame. Only four people knew where I would be that night. Terry Gleeson, Rachel, Alec Kendrick, and Sebastian Clark himself. The first three I could discount as having no reason to warn me off the investigation, the fourth was a distinct possibility. On the other hand, whoever wanted to keep my nose out of their business could easily have had me followed, and told their toughs to take their chance when they could. Between Birmingham and Leamington I'd not been alone at any time, so the only opportunity for my attackers would have been after I'd left the train and the main roads.

Next morning, I'd resolved nothing. Rachel was quiet, helping me to dress and get downstairs to our kitchen. She only spoke after she'd cleared the breakfast dishes and put them away.

'This is no good, James.' She swept a hand up the length of my body. 'You could have been killed last night. Look at the state you're in.'

'They didn't want to kill me. Just warn me off.'

'And have they? I expect not, you're so stubborn. So what about next time? Don't you see? Someone murdered Henry Dyer and left him in the park to rot. That will be you if you don't pack it in, and I'll be the wife waiting for you to come home, not knowing if you're dead in a deserted yard somewhere.'

I sighed and shook my head. 'We've been through this already, Rachel. Henry took me under his wing years ago and I owe him a lot. The least I can do is try to find his killer.'

Rachel turned and looked out of the window. 'As you say, we've been through this. And I meant what I said. You'll have to move out. I don't want to be around to get that visit from the police. I'll pack your bag, and you can go to stay with your parents until this is all over. If it ever is, and you come out alive, then we can talk about what happens next.'

'Rachel, you can't mean it —'

Her voice rose. 'I do, James. I rang your father last night and he agreed with me: you shouldn't be getting into this.'

'That's hardly a surprise, is it? I suppose he also suggested I should be satisfied spending my time working for him.'

'Actually, he didn't. And that's not what I want either.'

I tried to stand but winced with the pain and gave it up. 'So what do you suggest I should do, Rachel? Should I just walk away from finding Henry's murderer?'

'You know what I think, but you'll take no notice, so what's the point in repeating it? You do as you wish, but you'll not do it under this roof. Go to your parents' home and stay there. When you're ready to give it up, we can talk about you coming back. But you must stop. All of it. For good.'

Rachel was shaking when she finished, tears streaming down her face. I went to hold her, but she pushed me away. I sat again and stared at my shoelaces. After a few moments of near silence, she wiped her eyes on her pinafore hem and went through to the living room. She dialled a number, and I heard her talking to her brother, Bernard.

An hour later, he collected me and my bag in his car, then drove me to my parents' home. My mother fussed and implored me to take to my bed. I resisted until my eyes began to droop and my ribs responded to the painkillers, then I gave in. Before I dropped off, my father came through, stared at my cut and bruised face, tut-tutted and left again. As I drifted off, I swore I'd not stay under his roof for a moment longer than necessary.

Mama woke me with tea and drawn curtains at seven. I'd slept the whole afternoon and night. She sat on the bed, down by my feet, her face sombre.

'Papa is very angry with you, James. You know this, don't you?'

'Nothing new there then, is there, Mama?'

She ran a hand through her grey hair. 'Why can't you two get along? You were close when you were a boy, and I know he loves you.'

To be honest, I'd never known what made us argue so much. Perhaps it was the pride he'd displayed in my elder brother that had started the rot. I'd only been ten years of age when the last war had broken out and too young for the army. Ariel had paraded around the house and been so smart in his uniform before he left for the front. Papa talked about him for weeks, telling all his friends what a fine boy he had. Never plural — just the one.

After this, we'd seemed to quarrel all the time, until, a couple of years after the war had finished, I'd left one day for the sea and didn't return to Birmingham for years. Since then we'd tolerated each other, but only if we weren't together for too long. When we were, the arguments started. The only time we'd had a real truce was when Ariel was killed in Spain, still the hero, fighting for what he believed to be freedom.

'I know he loves me, Mama, and I love him, but that's not enough, is it?' I took a slurp from my cup. 'I'll have a word with him later, see if we can't patch it up.'

She went to prepare breakfast and I began to dress, wincing at the blue-black bruises in the wardrobe mirror. When I went through to the kitchen, my cousin, Anna, came through the door from the workshop, carrying a pillow and blankets. I asked where she'd been.

'I slept on a bench downstairs. You needed the bed.'

It hadn't occurred to me that my parents' rooms were so overcrowded. There had always seemed to be lots of space, but when I thought of it, it was obvious. Although a large building, split over three floors, much was taken up by the workshop and storage. They had a living room, parlour, kitchen and one bedroom on the first floor, then two decent bedrooms and a smaller one at the top.

When I'd been a boy there'd only been the four of us, so we'd had space to spare. Later, after I left and Ariel moved out, we were replaced by the younger ones, Eli and Sarah, so the home still wasn't overcrowded, even if one of us returned home for a while. Over the last couple of years my cousin Anna, my Aunt Miriam, and the refugee, Meena, had all moved in and needed to sleep somewhere. Eli had joined the army and relieved the pressure, but yesterday I'd turned up, expecting a bed.

'I'm so sorry, Anna. I didn't realise. You must have your room back. I'll take the bench tonight.'

'No, no, you mustn't. This is your home.'

I shook my head. 'Not for a long time. I'm a visitor here now. I'll not be staying long, perhaps only one more night, so downstairs will be no discomfort.'

After breakfast, I went down to face my father. He stood at his cutting table and stared down at a bolt of cloth when I arrived.

'Papa?'

He looked up. 'Yes?'

'I need to apologise.'

'I think you do.'

'Things haven't been great lately.'

'They're not great for anyone at the minute, Jacob. Half my workmen have been conscripted, and the women left behind are fine stitchers but struggle with the heavy jobs. The men who are here have brothers or sons in the army, and their minds are on the work only half the time. You've seen it upstairs. Six of us sharing four bedrooms, and me working all hours to earn enough to feed us all. Before we lost your Uncle Gideon, I'd been hoping to cut down. Perhaps not retiring, but not putting in quite so much time every day. But what could I do? He'd left a wife and daughter who needed our help, so we took them in. Then there's the worry of you.'

'You don't need to worry about me, Papa.'

'Hmm. I don't? That's easy for you to say. You'll always be my son, and look at the state you're in. With those bruises you'd win no beauty competitions this week, that's for sure. You're desperate to get away from here, you don't want the job I've provided, and you have nothing to replace it. And your lovely wife, she must be driven to distraction.'

His mention of Rachel did nothing to make me feel better.

'I'm sure you're right. That's why I need to go away again to sort things out. Just for a few more days in Leamington.'

My father sat down and slapped a hand to his forehead. 'You're doing what, Jacob? How will that solve anything? It will only make matters worse. Do you think I can keep a job open here for you whenever you want to leave town?'

'If I don't take the time it needs then it will drag on, a day here and a day there, and it's even more likely that Henry's killer will never be found. The sooner it's over, the sooner Rachel and I will get back together.'

'And the sooner you might get your head cracked open.'

We carried on for another ten minutes, with me trying to placate, and my father digging out his old grievances. In the end, I told him he'd not have to put up with me much longer, and that I would stay one more night before leaving for Leamington.

'I'll be gone for as long as it takes.'

Before he could reply, I hobbled away to my desk and tried to concentrate on the jobs which I needed to finish before the weekend. The only break I took was to telephone Alec Kendrick to ask if I could take up his offer of accommodation for a few days.

TWENTY

Friday 2nd August, 1940

In the evening, after our Sabbath meal, Anna gently argued again that I should keep her room, and I was just as insistent she should have it back. By half past one in the morning, with no sleep behind me and every bruised bone rebelling against the unforgiving workshop bench, I was beginning to wish I'd accepted her offer.

Each time I sank towards sleep, pictures of Henry drifted into view, his eyes staring, pleading with me to find who killed him. Even when I escaped this, Rachel hovered in front of my eyes, weeping over a coffin containing my corpse.

With every scrap of light excluded from the room by the blackout curtains, my mood sank into darkness. At times like this I'd often reached for the bottle, my age-old companion when times became tough, but one thing Rachel had taught me was that it didn't help. The last time had been in Brittany; I'd been so deep in despair I thought I'd never climb out without the lift from glasses of rum. Rachel had pulled me clear that night, not without some hurt on her part. I owed it to our marriage to keep a clear head and get through this without the booze.

All night I tossed and turned, eventually nodding off at around six, only to be woken at half past seven by a fire engine roaring past with bells blaring. I got up and shuffled past the tables and machines, all empty, as they always were on Saturday morning. Upstairs, my mother fussed and asked me to eat something before I left, but I told her I wasn't hungry. It only took a few minutes to pack my bag.

I left her with a promise that I'd be careful and look after myself, and I dragged my feet down the street until I reached St Philip's Cathedral. Here, the singing birds, the bright flowers exploding in the borders, and the shopworkers going about their business lifted my spirits. The morning air began to feel fresh and hopeful as I made my way across town to the railway station. I crossed my fingers in a childish gesture, hoping this would be my last trip to Leamington.

A man in his thirties answered my knock at Alec Kendrick's substantial Regency house. Framed in the wide, oak doorway, with coloured light streaming through a stunning stained-glass window at the other end of the hall, the man looked like a relic from the past. The cut of his jacket and shirt collar were at least thirty years out of date, similar to the ones my father tailored for me, despite my objections he should buy more modern patterns.

'Mr Given, is it? I'm Andrew Kendrick. Dad's had to take a business call. He's upstairs in his room but will be free shortly.' He glimpsed my walking stick and reached forward. 'Here, let me take your bag.'

I held up a palm and said I'd manage. Kendrick the Younger ran a hand through his curly hair, grinned and beckoned me into the high-ceilinged hall. Two portraits in ornate gilt frames faced each other across a substantial staircase. These, the maroon walls and the grand tiled floor, spoke of an owner with money, though the slightly flaking paint suggested it hadn't been done by the current generation. One of the paintings was undoubtedly Alec Kendrick.

'Is that you?'

'It is, a long time ago. I've been asking Dad to have a new one done now we're grown up, but he's not keen as it wouldn't include Mum.'

'She's no longer with you?'

'Died when I was ten, only a few years after that was done.'

'I'm sorry to hear that. It can't have been easy for your father, bringing you up on his own.'

'I don't believe it was. I tell him all the time how grateful I am, but he just brushes it off. He's the kindest, most Christian man I know.'

I glanced at the second group, a couple and a single child, and I recognised something familiar in the eyes of the tall, broad man at its centre. It reminded me of the photograph of my parents and my father's family I'd kept above the desk in my study for many of my bachelor years. There was nothing grand in my relic of the past; it recorded the hard life of Jewish peasants in a remote Russian village. The similarity lay in how the Kendrick family and my family kept alive memories of where we'd come from.

'Those are your grandparents, I assume.'

He laughed. 'It's easy to see you were a detective, Mr Given. My dad said you were good. Grandfather had that one done when his business began to be successful. They didn't have this house then, so I expect that enormous thing must have dominated their living room.'

At that moment, a door behind me swung open and my host came through.

'Ah, you're here.' Alec Kendrick stuck out a hand. 'Good to see you.'

'And you, Alec. It's very good of you to put me up like this.'

'Not at all, especially as you look like you've been in the wars. What happened?'

I explained I'd been jumped the last time I'd been in the town.

'How awful. That must have been very distressing. I don't think I would come back to Leamington after such a thing … though I'm glad you have, of course. Now, has my son been looking after you?'

'He has. We were talking about your family paintings. Nice to have such heirlooms, isn't it? I was trying to work out if you're more like your mother or your father.'

'I think it depends on the light. I like to believe I've a little of both of them. You'll perhaps see my father while you're staying. He has his own room at the other end of the house and doesn't come out much these days, but I might convince him to join us for a sherry one evening.' Kendrick looked at his watch. 'I'm afraid I must leave you to your own devices, James. I need to go in to the factory. Wheels of industry never stop and all that. Andrew will show you to your room, then you can come and go as you please. Dinner will be about seven.'

I thanked him again for his hospitality and followed his son upstairs, then along a corridor to the right. Andrew swung open the third door.

'This one's yours. The family rooms are the other side and we keep these for guests, not that we have many these days.'

The bedroom was almost the biggest I'd ever seen, though it looked like the decor and furnishings hadn't been changed since the house was built. As in the hall, the paintwork had faded, and damp had even peeled some of the gloss from the windowsill. I'd have guessed the armchair and bed had been bought many decades ago, and the dressing table long before then. If, as Andrew Kendrick had said, these were guest rooms and largely unused, then it would be understandable not to waste money on keeping them up to date. The only apparent concession to modernity was a large radiator on one wall, at odds with the handsome, though obsolete, tiled fireplace beside it.

I dropped my case by the bed and asked Andrew if I could use a telephone. He pointed with his thumb towards the door and said there was one in the hall where we'd just been. He then left me to it. I spent a few minutes hanging my clothes in a huge mahogany wardrobe then went to make my call. Clark answered after a couple of rings.

'Hello, Sebastian Clark speaking.'

'Good morning, sir, it's James Given. Would it be possible to see you today?'

He paused. 'Are you sure?'

'How do you mean?'

'Well, you stood me up the other evening, Mr Given. I waited in especially. I'm not used to having my time wasted in that way.'

I apologised and explained what had happened. He replied in a flat, uncommitted tone.

'Oh dear, I am sorry to hear that. You've obviously rubbed someone up the wrong way.'

'It seems like it. So are you free?'

'If you really must come round, then I suppose you better had. I've some paperwork I simply have to deal with first, so give me an hour.'

TWENTY-ONE

Saturday 3rd August, 1940

Clark led me to an office on the ground floor of the house. Even though the mahogany desk and filing cabinet confirmed it as a place of work, the leather armchairs and drinks cabinet showed that some of his clients required a more leisurely and informal approach to business transactions. He offered me a seat by the desk and took his on the other side. We were to be formal. Clark peered over the rim of his glasses, took a single sheet of paper from a drawer, and lay his fountain pen on top.

'When we spoke on the telephone last Tuesday, Mr Given, you said you were looking into the death of Mr Dyer. Can I ask what your interest is in this matter?'

'He used to be my boss; more recently, he'd become a friend. I discovered his body.'

There wasn't a flicker of shock.

'So how can I help you? I didn't know the man very well.'

'I'm told you knew him well enough to have a row not long before he was killed.'

'Who told you that?'

'You were seen at the golf club. It doesn't matter who told me. Is it true?'

'We had a disagreement. I might have spoken a little more strongly than was appropriate in the circumstances.'

'And what were those circumstances?'

'I'm sorry, Mr Given, but that's confidential.'

I gave him the standard response. 'Nothing is private in a murder investigation, Mr Clark. The police will tell you that.' I pointed to his telephone. 'If you telephone the local station and ask for Inspector Moore, I'm sure he'll confirm what I say.'

Clark sighed. 'We'd talked about an investment, and Dyer pulled out at the last minute. I wasn't happy, and I told him so.'

'You were heard to threaten him.'

'I didn't threaten him.'

'It's been said you told him he'd be sorry.'

Clark laughed. 'A manner of speech, that's all, not a threat. I meant he'd be sorry not to have taken advantage of the investment.'

'Really? Is that all?'

'Well, I'd also told him he'd not get investment advice from anyone again if he didn't go ahead.' Clark rubbed his forehead. 'Look, Mr Given, it takes a good deal of time to set these deals up. I'd had to put some money up front with the parties involved, cash I couldn't afford to lose.'

I looked round the office, showing him I'd taken in its opulence. 'It doesn't look to me like you're a man on the breadline, Mr Clark.'

'I'd not attract many clients if I did, would I? Don't mistake the window dressing for anything more than it is. I'm not destitute, but I try to make my money work for me, rather than piling it up in the bank. Most businesses do the same. I'd stretched my liquid cash to the limit, then Dyer messed me about. Right up to the last minute he'd said he wanted to go ahead then, for some reason, he got cold feet.'

'Would you say you're a vindictive man?'

'In what way?'

'It's not a difficult question. Did Henry's refusal to proceed make you angry enough for you to take revenge?'

'What? No. Usually I'd smile and walk away, put it down to experience and hope for another commission when the client sees sense. Admittedly, this one had put me under a lot of pressure and I wasn't pleased, but I'd not hurt someone over it. Better to put my energy into finding a replacement investor, which I did. I'd forgotten the argument five minutes after I left the clubhouse.' Clark started to rise from his seat. 'So, is there anything else?'

I flipped a few pages through my notepad. 'I do have another two questions. Is that all right?'

He settled down again. 'Fine, but please make it quick. I've work to do.'

'Can I ask where you were on Monday morning, three weeks ago? The fifteenth of July. Say, between eleven o'clock and one o'clock?'

'I'll have to look at my appointments. Give me a minute.' Clark opened his desk diary. 'Monday, you say? Here it is. I was with my bank manager in Warwick. Trying to confirm an overdraft, as it happens, to get me through the mess Dyer had left. Afterwards I met Donald Quinn, my business partner, for lunch, also in Warwick. We'd a lot to discuss, so it was a long one and I arrived back here sometime after three. I'm sure they'll both confirm I'm telling the truth, if you give them a call. Now, what's your final question?'

'Only four people knew I was meeting you last week. My wife, two others who had no interest in preventing me coming here, and you. Did you pay those thugs to beat a tattoo on my ribs?'

Sebastian Clark stared at me for a minute. 'You don't really expect me to dignify that with an answer, do you, Mr Given?' He stood, walked round to the office door, and swung it open. 'I think it's time you were going now, don't you?'

I rose slowly, trying to show I wouldn't be bullied. In the hall, he reached to turn the door handle, but I covered his hand and stopped him.

'Let's be clear, Mr Clark: I'm not entirely convinced by what you've told me here today, and I may be back with more questions in due course.'

He smiled a predator's smile. 'Well, you're more than welcome to call any time, Mr Given, but make sure you telephone in advance so I can inform my solicitor. And perhaps you should actually bring one of your policeman friends next time.'

Outside, the heat was splitting the pavement, so I wandered over the river and to the park cafeteria where I ordered tea and sandwiches. Basking in the sunshine, surrounded by genteel elderly couples, uniformed nannies, and mothers with infants occupying the nearby tables, I found it hard to believe there could be enough evil in the world to cause wars, and for a murder to be committed within a few hundred yards of where I was sitting.

After the waitress, in a blue dress and starched white apron, brought my food and drink, I settled to consider what had just happened in Clark's office. His reaction might suggest he knew something of the attack on me, or it could simply be annoyance at being accused when he was innocent. I didn't like him, but that didn't mean he was a criminal.

I took my time over lunch, mulling over possibilities and watching the activity in the park, then wandered back to Alec's house. Their maid, Clarrie, let me in.

'Good afternoon, sir. There's been a telephone call for you, a Mister Gleeson.' She fetched a slip of paper from the hall table and passed it to me. 'He left his number and asked if you could call him as soon you returned.'

I took the note and went to the phone. 'Terry? You rang.'

'I made a couple of calls after you left. I couldn't find a recent address for Derek Taylor, but I did find one for his ex-wife. She divorced him when he was inside and is still living in Leamington. If you go round there, she might know where her old man's moved to. Worth a shot, anyway.'

I thanked him and took down the details, then went and asked Clarrie if she knew where it was, assuming she'd know the poorer parts of town better than my host. I was right, and she gave me clear directions to get there in ten minutes or so. Before I left, I made a call to Clark's bank manager. He was busy, but I left a message saying that I needed him to confirm an appointment his customer claimed to have had some weeks earlier.

Derek Taylor's wife was my height, tall for a woman. Two cats, one tabby and one black, rubbed against her ankles, and stared up at me. She squinted short-sightedly when she spoke.

'Can I 'elp you?'

'Mrs Taylor, is it?'

'Who wants to know?'

'My name's James Given. I'm looking for your husband.'

'I haven't got no 'usband.'

'I suppose I should have said your ex-husband, Derek Taylor. Do you know where he is?'

'He's not 'ere. Lives on a farm now, 'tween 'ere and Warwick.'

I asked if she knew where it was exactly and she told me. She said they were still in touch.

'We've become quite good friends again, now we're not married,' she laughed. 'Must be because 'e got religion. Give 'im my regards when you see 'im.'

I thanked Mrs Taylor and hurried back to the house to ask Andrew Kendrick if there was any chance of a lift to Mr Taylor's home.

Twenty-five minutes later, most of which had been spent by Andrew trying to locate his father's road map, we pulled in to a farm gate. The car stopped beside a cart stacked with bales of hay, being unloaded by a bald man in overalls and wellington boots. I climbed out of the car, narrowly avoiding a fresh cowpat and wishing I'd had the foresight to borrow suitable footwear.

'I'm looking for a Derek Taylor, sir. Does he work here?'

The man stepped back from his work and eyed me suspiciously. 'I'm Taylor. What do you want?'

'Nothing to worry about, Mr Taylor. I just have a few questions. Can you spare me a minute?'

'You police?'

I shook my head. 'No, I'm not.'

He jerked his thumb in the direction of a barn. 'You'd best come in there, then. I can't be long; the boss will be none too pleased if I don't get this lot finished.'

Inside, three quarters of the space was stacked to the corrugated iron roof with bales from a recent cutting, and Taylor indicated for me to sit where I could. He pulled a half-smoked cigarette from his top pocket, lit up and took a deep drag.

'Now, what can I do for you, Mr...?'

I told him my name. 'Could we begin with me asking how long you've worked here?'

'About nine months.'

'And before that you were in Strangeways?'

Taylor took the cigarette from his mouth and spat a speck of tobacco on the ground. 'Who told you that?'

'Through an ex-colleague of mine, Sergeant Baines. Do you know him?'

'I thought you said you weren't a copper.'

'I'm not, not anymore. So, you were in Strangeways before here?'

'Yes.'

'We have someone else in common, then. Superintendent Henry Dyer.'

He jumped up and glared. 'You know him?'

'I did. He's dead.'

The fight went out of Taylor as quickly as it had boiled up, and he sat down, his brows knitted in a puzzled frown. 'Dead? The good Lord forgive me, but I thank him for that.'

'You're pleased he's dead, then?'

'The man put me away for twenty years, and I'd done nothing. A fight that went too far, that's all. What would any man have done if he'd found his wife running round with another bloke, I ask you?'

'Henry Dyer didn't find you guilty, it was the judge and jury. Still, it sounds like you've kept a grudge for all this time. Enough to kill him when you got out?'

'What? No. Is that what you're here for? To fit me up, like he did?'

'I've no interest in fitting you up, as you put it. I want to find who did it, that's all, and your name has come up.'

'Well, it wasn't me. When I was inside, I had a lot of time to think. I lost my wife, my friends, everything, but what saved me from going under was the Bible.'

I raised an eyebrow.

'It's true, Mr Given. I raged and raged when they first locked me up. Paced my cell night after night. Fought with other prisoners and the warders. Then one day, when I'd had a good thumping for my trouble, the chaplain came to see me. Asked me to read some verses from Saint Matthew's gospel and, you know, they made sense. He came every week after that and we read together. Calmed me right down, it did. I got a new way of looking at things. After a year or more, I can't say I completely forgave Dyer, not like the Lord says we should, but I didn't want to hurt him no more.'

I'd seen this before in ex-prisoners. Whether it was a real conversion to religion, or just having time to reflect on their misspent lives, I didn't know, but sometimes they came out better men.

'Have you anyone who can vouch for where you were when Henry Dyer was killed?' I gave him the date. 'I think an alibi might be more effective than God at the minute.'

Taylor asked me to wait, and ambled off to the house next to the barn. He returned after a few minutes with an older man in a brown tweed suit. He introduced himself as Taylor's boss.

'Derek's asked me to tell you where he was on Monday, three weeks ago. Well, I can tell you, definitely, he was with me.'

'You're certain?'

'Not a doubt. On alternate Mondays there's a livestock market in Stratford. We're up at the crack of dawn to load the trailer and get down there for breakfast. Finishes at about one and we have a bite to eat and a jar, then back. Never home much before three. Then we put away anything I've bought and clean up. Afterwards, we have to catch up on the rest of the day's work.' He glanced at Taylor. 'Never much rest round a farm, is there, Derek?' The farmer walked over to Taylor and put a hand on his shoulder. 'I know this lad's had his troubles, but that's all past him now. He's a fine worker and goes to church every Sunday, so that makes him good in my book. Derek said you suspect him of something, but I'd bet he didn't do anything bad. He's not got it in him anymore.'

TWENTY-TWO

Monday 5th August, 1940

I could do nothing on Sunday to progress the case. The bank was closed and Donald Quinn, Clark's business partner, wasn't answering his telephone. Alec knew of a couple of farms which might be of interest in my house-hunt, so Andrew drove me to have a look. Although they were both much bigger than Rachel and I could afford, Andrew was good company and we stopped off at a pub by the river. We chatted about our families, and he asked if I had any brothers or sisters. I told him I had two brothers and a sister, though one of my brothers had been killed in Spain.

'How awful.'

'Every day I wish I'd been able to save him, but I wasn't there. Ariel was a much braver man than I'll ever be.'

'I'm sure if I had a brother I'd do anything to stop something bad happening to them. Brothers should be close, don't you think?'

I agreed and we went on to talk about his hopes and fears for the family business, until it was time to leave. Later, I spent the day eating, napping after dinner, and chatting to father and son in their garden.

On Monday morning I rang the bank as soon as it opened, to check on Clark's alibi. The manager said he'd need to get permission from Clark to discuss such sensitive information, so I walked into town to buy a newspaper. When I got back, he'd left a message to call and, unsurprisingly, the manager was able to confirm Clark had been with him when he'd said.

As a further check, I telephoned Donald Quinn again, and this time he answered. I asked if he knew Clark's movements on the relevant date.

'Mr Clark said you and he had lunch on that Monday — is that correct?'

'I believe so. We get together once a month to go through our figures, talk about new opportunities, that kind of thing.'

'He says he was with you at about twelve, Mr Quinn. Would that be right?'

'That's the time we usually meet, yes. I spend the morning preparing and making sure the day's work is out of the way. I have to confess it's our treat. A good meal and a glass or two taken, so there's not much done in the afternoon when we get back to base.'

'And this particular day was no different?'

Quinn paused and I heard paper shuffling at the end of the line. 'Wait a minute. I'm sorry, Mr Given, but I've just checked my diary and there's a note scribbled in the margin. I missed it a minute ago. I'd had a message earlier in the day from a client wanting to move his appointment back an hour. I knew Sebastian would understand, he'd do the same, so I let him know and we met at one instead.'

'You met later?'

'As I say, it's not that unusual. We try to stick to a regular time, but if there's a potential sale we both understand and make allowances. I knew he'd be at the bank that morning, so I left a message for him there.'

'Any idea what Mr Clark did with the extra hour?'

'Yes, now I remember it, he said he'd wandered around town window shopping, then popped into a café for tea and a slice of cake. We had a laugh about it because I said I didn't know where he put it all, especially before a three-course lunch.'

Donald Quinn's account put a very different complexion on Clark's story. Warwick to Leamington would take around ten minutes by car. Allowing for walking at each end, Clark could easily have left the bank, driven to meet Henry Dyer, and still have made it back for his lunch appointment, in less than an hour.

When I asked Quinn if he was sure of the timings, and if he was happy what his business partner had told him was true, he fell quiet for a moment. It seemed I'd touched a nerve.

'Now listen, Mr Given, I'm not used to discussing my business affairs in this manner and have only done so because I thought it would help Sebastian. If you're going to twist what I say to lay blame at his door, then this discussion is over. I've known the man for years; we were at school together, for God's sake, and though he may cut a few corners now and then, he's honest at heart. And he's not a liar. What exactly is it you think he's done?'

'I'm surprised your friend hasn't told you. Why do you think that is?'

Quinn spluttered. 'I've not a clue.'

'You've been very helpful, Mr Quinn, but I need to ask you one final question. With all your years' knowledge of Mr Clark, would you say he could be a violent man?'

'Sebastian? Violent? Not a chance.'

I hung up.

Clark hadn't known he'd be free until he was already in Warwick, but he could have spotted the opportunity of an alibi and phoned his victim to meet him. However, for this theory to work, he could only have made the call soon after arriving at the bank, and before Henry left the house for his walk. A very small window — minutes, though possible. If Clark had offered an even better return on the investment, which needed to be acted upon quickly, this may have prompted Henry to put aside their argument and agree to meet. On the downside, neither Clark's bank manager, nor Audrey, had mentioned a telephone conversation between the pair that morning.

I'd had cases where money was at the heart of a murder, but none where it was simply the loss of a commission. Clark may have wanted revenge, but this would be a little extreme. Henry probably wasn't the first client he'd lost, and I had nothing to suggest he'd committed a string of killings related to failed investment opportunities. Clark had even said he'd found someone to replace Henry anyway, so he wouldn't have been out of pocket by much. But then, why had he lied about the time he'd met with Quinn?

Sebastian Clark answered his telephone with his most ingratiating voice, then became curt when he heard it was me. 'I don't wish to speak to you, Mr Given, not if you're going to make baseless accusations.'

'I'm sorry, Mr Clark. I'm not making an accusation, but I do need to clarify something with you. I hope you understand why I'm asking these questions.'

'Frankly, I don't. I hardly knew Henry Dyer, and we didn't really get on. So, though I wished him no harm, his death is of little consequence to me. You seem hell-bent on linking me to his murder, a ridiculous notion. Why should I tell you any more than I already have?'

'We've been through this before. You were seen arguing with Henry and then he turned up dead. You have to accept this might be of interest to the police, and if I were to mention it to them, they'd be round to your house quickly enough. All I'm asking is that you tell me what I need to know, then it need go no further.'

He waited a long time to answer, so long I thought we'd lost the connection.

'Mr Clark?'

'Sorry, I was thinking. What else can I tell you, Mr Given? I gave you my whereabouts last time we spoke.'

'That's the problem, really. It seems there was quite a big gap between you leaving the bank and meeting your partner — at least an hour, maybe more.'

'How so?'

'The information I have is that Mr Quinn had another appointment that morning and asked you to meet him later, at one. This is important in relation to where you were, and you forgot to mention it.'

'What can I say? You're right. I forgot. The change wasn't in my diary because I was already in Warwick when Donald sent word he'd be late. It had gone completely out of my head until I was mulling over our conversation after you'd left this morning. I considered letting you know, but I haven't had a chance yet.'

'So where were you?'

'Donald's message was passed to me when I arrived at the bank a few minutes before eleven. There was a lot for the manager and I to discuss, so I left at around quarter to twelve. I wandered around the town for a short while then went to a café on Market Place.'

I asked him which one.

'It's called the Cosy Kettle, I believe. I usually go in there, or in one of the hotels.'

'They'd confirm you were there?'

'I doubt they know my name, but they'd possibly recognise me. I only had a pot of tea, so they'd have no reason to remember the time, or even the day. You can ask, though I doubt it would stand up in court.'

'Would it have to?'

'You tell me, Mr Given. I'm a respectable businessman, and you're asking me all sorts of questions, insinuating I'm a criminal. I have to assume that at some point you hope to get me in court.'

'Only if I have good cause, Mr Clark. Only if I have good cause.'

There'd be very little chance of putting Sebastian Clark in the dock, unless I could come up with something more concrete than a late appointment, an argument with the victim, and the inability of an overworked waitress to vouch for him. Even the time window which meant he could have committed the murder was only circumstantial. If he'd driven back to Leamington, he could still have had time to nip into the café he'd named, and they'd have been so busy at lunchtime they'd hardly have noticed which customers came in, and when.

Would Clark have been so smart as to think on the spot of something impossible to dispute? I'd need to keep him on my list of potentials for the time being.

Stephen Grainger lived in a neat, semi-detached house in Leamington which would have been almost new when his wife, Christine, had been arrested. It had a bay window, a stucco white-painted front, and a well-stocked, if a little overgrown, garden entirely in keeping with respectable suburbia. Not in the same league as Alec Kendrick's, Sebastian Clark's, or Henry's, but still very nice. It was easy to see how it might be assumed the Graingers were living beyond their means when the wife was suspected of embezzlement and manslaughter.

I'd discovered from reading up on the court case that the husband had held down two jobs, plus, it was claimed, he had something of a golden touch when it came to gambling on the horses. Christine's defence rested on the cash which enabled them to buy the house coming from a particularly spectacular run of wins at Aintree, though no-one could be brought forward to substantiate this story. In the absence of corroboration, and considering her easy access to the company's bank account, Christine was convicted of both charges and sentenced to life, though she had been let out after twenty years. It would have been longer, possibly even with the death penalty, if the prosecution could have proved she'd known her manager would have been inside the building when she'd set it alight.

There'd been discrepancies in the case against Grainger, not least because payments into her bank account didn't match, in date or amount, the losses from the company account. This was discounted on the basis she could have had another account which hadn't been found, or she'd spent some of the cash and banked the rest when she thought it safe to do so. Stephen Grainger had fought his wife's conviction for years on these disparities, without success.

When he opened his front door, I could see the toll it had taken on him. A tall man, his brown suit hung limp on his frame, and dark eyes sunk in a grey face. His most striking feature, jet-black hair with a white shock down the left side, looked unwashed and uncombed. I found it difficult to imagine this specimen organising a complicated legal defence. He leant on the doorframe.

'Yes?'

The booze on his breath nearly knocked me over. I introduced myself and asked if we might go inside.

'What for? Do I know you?' His words were slurred.

'I need to talk to you about your wife, Mr Grainger. It really would be better if we didn't do this in the street.'

He straightened himself to his full height. 'Nothing to talk about. She's gone.'

'I know she has. That's why I'm here.'

Grainger turned, leant his back against the wall, and swung a palm to wave me into the hall. 'You'd better come in, then.'

He shut the door, more loudly than if he'd been sober, and I let him pass to lead me to his front room. Other than a thin layer of dust on a table and sideboard against one wall, there was no hint a man lived here alone. No clutter, and the furniture appeared hardly used. The only thing breaking the impression of a neat and orderly home was the half empty bottle of whisky on the mantelpiece and the half full glass next to it. Grainger ambled over and toasted the glass in my direction.

'Will you join me, Mr ... er ... Given?'

I refused and sat down on the sofa. Grainger leaned back in an armchair opposite, closing his eyes.

'So, what can I do for you?'

'I heard Mrs Grainger died recently.'

'She did. Wonderful woman.'

'When was this?'

Grainger opened his eyes and peered at me. 'About three months ago. Why?'

'Just trying to get an idea of events.' I thought I'd fly a kite. 'Was this when you started damaging Henry Dyer's house?'

For a drunk he was up and towering over me astonishingly fast, with fists clenched at his sides. I held his glare, and after a long minute he stepped back. Grainger raised a shaking arm and pointed to the door. 'Get out, damn you, get out. How dare you come in here, asking questions like that.'

I stood and walked to the front door, then turned and looked back. 'I'll go now, Mr Grainger, but I'll be back in an hour with the police. Don't go anywhere, will you?'

TWENTY-THREE

Monday 5th August, 1940

I arrived back on Stephen Grainger's doorstep in less than an hour, this time with two constables in tow, to make sure he came along to Leamington police station for Bob Moore's questioning.

Bob hadn't hesitated in agreeing to bring Grainger in for a chat. He'd read the file on the man's wife. Bob waited at the station until we brought the suspect in, so we could interview him together.

Grainger offered no resistance, and he'd sobered up quite a bit since I'd left him. He joked with the two officers as he walked between them into town, but he became quieter when we arrived on the steps of the police station. Inside, I didn't need the men any longer, and I asked the desk sergeant to point me in the direction of the interview room we'd be using. As we walked towards it, the sergeant rang upstairs for Bob Moore to join us.

The interview room was not the one where I'd previously been questioned by Bob, though it would be hard to describe any differences, other than the position of the window. The walls were just as grey, the wooden furniture just as sparse. Within a couple of minutes, Bob had joined us and taken his position on a seat opposite Grainger. He went through the formalities, confirming name and address, as well as telling Grainger he was being questioned in relation to the murder of ex-Superintendent Henry Dyer on the fifteenth of July. When Grainger heard this caution, he stood up abruptly.

'What are you talking about? Murdered Dyer? Me?'

Moore showed a coolness I hadn't expected when he looked up into Grainger's eyes. 'Do sit down, Mr Grainger. There's no way out of here until I say you can go, and I'll not be doing any such thing until we've had our little chat. Now, I can leave, and you'll stay here for a few hours to calm down, or we can get on with it now. Which do you prefer?'

Grainger glanced at me, then at the door, then at Bob. Without a word he shook his head and sat down again, interlocking his fingers on the table.

'Go ahead then, Inspector. You can ask your questions, but if I think you're twisting my words, I'll want a solicitor here. I've seen how you coppers operate.'

Bob asked the obvious question. 'So you've been in trouble with us before?'

'No, I haven't. But I know damn well you had your claws in my wife. That Dyer questioned me but couldn't make anything stick. Not like with my Chrissy. Put two and two together there and made five. She hadn't a chance.'

'So it would be fair to say you bore a grudge against Superintendent Dyer.'

'Look, Inspector, you're doing it already.'

'Doing what?'

'Implying I killed him for what he'd done.'

'Well, did you?'

I looked at Grainger's hands. His knuckles were white, though he replied calmly.

'No, I didn't. Superintendent Dyer did what he had to do, investigating a serious theft and a sad death. Chrissy's employer was an important man in this town, still is, and he pulled all the strings he could to get a quick conviction. Personally, I think it was him who had his finger in the pie, but I've never managed to prove it, just like I've never been able to prove Chrissy's innocence. Once they'd seen she and I had been able to put by a bob or two, everyone, from Dyer up to the chief constable, convinced themselves she'd pinched the cash then set fire to the building to cover her tracks. Not one of them knew her. If they had, they'd be certain she could never do such a thing.'

Bob questioned Grainger about where he was on the morning Henry was killed. He said he'd been at work and gave details of his boss, who'd be able to confirm it.

I asked Bob if I could take over for a minute, and he nodded his agreement.

'If you had nothing to do with this murder, Mr Grainger, why were you so angry when I mentioned the damage to Henry Dyer's home?'

He looked towards the window and didn't answer.

'Come on, Stephen, you must have had a reason to throw me out of your house. What else are we supposed to think, other than that you have something to hide?'

Grainger lifted a hand and rubbed his forehead. 'Listen, Chrissy had just died and I was out of my mind. Some days I started drinking and wasn't always thinking straight. You have to believe that I didn't blame Dyer, but when you're grieving with booze inside you, you get mixed up. God forgive me, but I found out where he lived and I went round a few nights. Mostly I stood across the road and watched. Once or twice I crept into his garden and broke a plant pot, or such like. Nothing serious.'

'You poisoned his dog.'

'I know, I know. That's what made me stop. I'd been on the whisky all day and stumbled on some stuff in my shed. Said "dangerous to animals" on the box, and the idea hit me. I went round to Dyer's with a bit of meat smothered in the stuff and threw it over the fence. It was only when I woke next morning I realised it wasn't something to be proud of. All I wanted was for Dyer to be a bit rattled, to get it into his head that someone knew where he lived, and could get to him if they wanted. The dog, I admit, was a step too far. I didn't try to kill it, just make it sick, but still, not a nice thing to do to an animal. I wanted to go round and apologise then, but I lost my nerve.'

Bob made a note on his pad, then pointed a thumb at the door for us to go outside. In the corridor, he sighed.

'I'm sorry, James. I'm not sure I believe him, but we'll have to let him go. He has an alibi, which of course I'll check, and it's not worth the paperwork to do him over some petty vandalism.'

I had to agree with him. I'd have done the same. We agreed he'd check Grainger's alibi and I apologised for wasting his time.

'Not at all, James. You did what you thought best, but I have to say, if you'd make your mind up about rejoining us, this might be a whole lot easier.'

'Another apology, then, Bob. I've thought about it long and hard, and I'm not sure it's a good idea. It would only be temporary, until this case is finished, and that would hardly be fair on you or your boss.'

What I didn't tell him was that if I accepted the position, there'd be a good chance I would not see Rachel again.

I hadn't seen Audrey Dyer since I'd left Leamington after Henry's funeral, so I took a walk after dinner and found her in the garden, dead-heading her roses.

'Oh, good evening, James. Just doing some tidying up. Henry loved his flowers, you know, especially these. He'd always say, "The more you remove the spent ones, the more the stronger ones will come back — a bit like villains." I need to keep on top of them — only thing keeping me sane at the minute.'

I smiled at the thought of Henry's comment on the flowers; it was just like him to compare criminals with plants that needed a little pruning, whereas my experience told me more drastic action was sometimes required.

Even in the three weeks since Henry had died, the lawns bore no comparison to the perfection I'd seen on my first visit.

'Will you get a man in to help, Audrey?'

'Perhaps.' She looked round the borders. 'I'll never manage all this on my own, but I can't bear the idea of anyone taking Henry's place.'

'No-one can take his place, Audrey, but someone might be able to take on the jobs you can't handle.'

'You're right, James. Here, let me get you a drink. Tea? Lemonade? I know not to offer you gin. You don't mind if I have one, though, do you?'

I told her the lemonade would be welcome, and followed her into the house. A rib twinged as I reached across to pick up my glass and I winced.

'Are you all right, James? It looked like you were in pain.'

'I was beaten up last week. Mostly healed now, but still getting the odd niggle.'

'How awful. Do you know who did it?'

'I've not a clue. Someone trying to keep my nose out of their business. It was only a couple of heavies who did the job. I didn't know them, but I imagine they were paid to warn me off. Nothing personal on their part, and they're probably long gone by now.'

'Do you think it is linked with Henry's killing?'

The only men I'd ever known to hold a grudge against me had both died a year earlier, and even though I'd inevitably made enemies when I was on the force, I couldn't see any of them coming after me now I'd left.

'It must be. I'm not investigating anything else.'

Audrey slapped her hand over her mouth. 'Could they come after me?'

'I see no reason why they would. You're not the one asking the questions.'

'I ask questions all the time, James, like why has Henry been taken from me? What did we do to deserve this? I even asked the vicar, but all he said was that it must have been God's will.'

'Those are a different type of question, Audrey, and not likely to threaten the killer. No, I've touched a nerve somewhere. That's why I was attacked.'

The fear which had landed on her face for a moment faded. She drained her glass and offered to top up my lemonade. I refused and said I should be going, but she asked me to stay for a another minute, then left the room. When she returned, she carried a faded blue envelope.

'Could you take a look at this, James?'

She handed it over and I extracted a letter. A neat hand, with no return address, but dated more than sixty years earlier.

Dear Ellen,

Further to our recent discussion, the payments for our arrangement will continue for fourteen years or until a year after you marry, whichever is the sooner. In the event that I die before either of those come to fruition, I have left provision in my will to continue until the conditions are satisfied.

Edwin

'This is to Henry's mother?'

'It was with her things. I've been sorting them out to pass the time, and I found it last night.'

'Do you know the sender, Audrey?'

'We know a couple of men called Edwin, but this is written so long ago it wouldn't have been either of them. It's from before Henry or I were born. What can it mean?'

'I don't know. The wording is very precise, almost like a contract, but drawn up without the help of a solicitor. As if it's not quite legal. Was there anything else with it?'

'I found it in a jewellery box with some bits and pieces. Nothing valuable — a locket, a pretty silver bracelet, that kind of thing.'

'Do you know if Henry saw the letter?'

'I shouldn't think so, though he might have. He brought a lot of his mother's stuff here after she died. Perhaps that's what he had on his mind when I thought he seemed distracted.'

'I expect we'll never know. Do you mind if I take it away with me? I can't see what it could have to do with his murder — it's so long ago, as you say — but we've got to explore all avenues, I suppose.'

Audrey said she'd be glad if I took it; she had too much to go through already. 'As if it hasn't been enough to sort out Ellen's house and all her things, I now have Henry's to go through.' She sniffed and squeezed her eyes shut. 'It's been so difficult. Heaven knows what I'll do with all his clothes, James. He was such a big man, and men they'd fit would be few and far between.'

I looked away, and a photograph of a woman on the dresser, clearly not Audrey, caught my eye. 'Is that Henry's mother?'

'Yes, it is. Attractive woman, wasn't she?'

'Very much so. I can see Henry in her.'

'That's what I always used to say.'

I stood and tucked the letter into my wallet, then left Audrey to her thoughts. The sun had dropped below the rooftops, and those people still on the streets were hurrying to get home, avoiding being outside in the complete darkness of the blackout.

Ellen Dyer's letter occupied my mind as I wandered the half mile back to Alec Kendrick's house. Whoever had written it would now be dead or extremely old. No match for Henry in any kind of scuffle, so hardly a suspect.

TWENTY-FOUR

Monday 5th August, 1940

Alec and Andrew were sitting in the conservatory when I arrived at the house, the father relaxing in a wicker chair with a cigar and what looked like a brandy, the son reading an Agatha Christie paper-backed novel. The setting sun bathed the room in light to warm the soul, so I asked if I could join them. Alec picked up his glass and stood.

'We're coming inside now, James. We've almost lost the sun, and my father promised to come down when he heard we have a guest. He's always been a sociable man, but at his age he can't get out much these days.'

I stood aside and let them through, then followed Alec to a drawing room, while Andrew went upstairs to tell his grandfather I'd come back. The grand piano dominating one corner would have had Rachel drooling at its elegance, not to mention the oak panelling, deep maroon carpet and leather settees. We didn't think we were short of space in our home, but I guessed our whole ground floor would fit in this one room. Alec waved me to a seat then wandered over to the piano and tinkled at the keys for a moment. He drained and refilled his glass from a tray on top of an elegant walnut writing bureau.

'Will you have something, James?'

'Not for me, thanks. Do you play?'

'The piano? No, not really. Father paid for lessons when I was a boy, but I never quite took to it.'

'I should ask my wife, Rachel, to give you some. She's an excellent teacher. Plays half a dozen instruments and toured the world with an orchestra. I'm more than jealous.'

'I think I'm perhaps a little too old now, James, though it's a very kind offer. I never took to much, if the truth were known. Mediocre at school and university, and I worked in the family business most of my life, so I never had to fight to keep a job. I play golf mainly to keep contact with clients — can't say I'm much good at it. Being a rubbish player is a bit of an advantage, I suppose — wouldn't catch many contracts if I beat all the customers. I do envy people like you, who are good at what they do.'

I was about to tell him not to put himself down, when the door clattered, forced open by a walking stick in a mottled and wrinkled hand. The man, about twenty-five years Alec's senior, was bent almost double, and it was only when he came closer that I could see his face. He was bald, drawn and lined, but unmistakeably Alec's father. My host introduced him as Edwin Kendrick. He squinted through thick glasses.

'You're the policeman?' A wheezing, commanding voice.

'I was.'

'Why?'

'Why was I a policeman, or why did I stop?'

'The first.'

'Because someone I loved was murdered.'

'You're one of the selfish ones, then?'

'How so?'

'In my experience, men join the police for different reasons. Some because they love the power, some because they foolishly think they can keep the world safe, and others, like you, do it for vengeance. I'm assuming you left once you'd caught the men who'd wronged you. So you see, you're selfish, not power-hungry or idealistic. None is more laudable than the others; I just wanted to know what type of man I'm talking to.'

I was about to tell him he held a dim view of the police when Alec interrupted.

'Now, Father, no need to be unpleasant when you've only just met. What does the Bible say? Do unto others, and so on. Come and sit down.'

He took the old man by the elbow and guided him to a leather armchair, where Kendrick Senior collapsed, his eyes now on a level with mine. He laughed, bringing on a hoarse, phlegmy cough.

'I'm sorry, Mr Given, just my little bit of fun. This damned chest of mine makes me sound much more bad-tempered than I am. You're very welcome in our home, and I'm grateful for the favour you performed for young Alec.'

I had to smile, his son being almost twice my age. 'It was nothing. I was happy to help.'

'Still, it got us out of a jam. Business is hard enough these days without people stealing our ideas for the competition.' He turned to Alec. 'Can a man get a drink around here?'

'What would you like?'

'I'll have what you're having. Brandy, is it?'

Alec shook his head. 'You'll not have brandy, Father, it's not good for you. Would you like a soda? Or I could fetch lemonade from the kitchen.'

Edwin Kendrick started to shake. 'Fetch me a brandy, damn you. I'll not be told at my age what I can and can't have. Do you think it makes the slightest difference? I'll be dead soon enough anyway.'

I thought for a moment that Alec Kendrick was about to refuse, but the venom in his father's face told both of us he'd be well advised to take it no further. He poured a drop into a tumbler and passed it over. Edwin scowled and knocked it back in one.

'Another.'

'Father?'

'Another, I said, and make it a decent one this time. Then we can all have a nice chat.'

What followed was far from nice. For an hour, Alec attempted to make conversation and his father would snipe, belittling him with insults at every turn, this process punctuated by demands for more drink. Most of his jibes insinuated his son couldn't run the business successfully, a business the father had built over many years, but this wasn't his only complaint.

More than once I attempted to make my excuses and escape to bed, but Alec almost begged me to stay a little longer. The ridiculing continued with no reaction from him, other than trying to placate Edwin Kendrick, until an exchange seemed to hit a nerve, started innocently enough by me. They'd talked for a few minutes, peacefully enough, about how the military contracts looked to be providing some financial security for the company, and I thought the alcohol had finally mellowed the older man. He even nodded and muttered, 'Well done.'

'That must make you proud of your son, Mr Kendrick.'

Edwin raised his head and peered at me. 'My son?' His words were slurred and he raised a wavering hand from his lap, pointing in Alec's direction. 'Ha! You mean him? He's no son of mine. He's —'

Alec was on his feet and towering over his father in a flash. 'Don't you dare say another word. Shut up. Just shut up.'

Edwin closed his mouth slowly, then laughed to himself, before raising his glass and demanding a refill.

'You'll have no more, Father. I'll call Andrew to help you to your bed.'

The younger man arrived and took his grandfather by the arm. Edwin pulled it away, scowling and swearing in the foulest manner I'd heard outside the police cells. Andrew grabbed him again, more firmly this time. Alec also took hold, and despite his struggling, Edwin couldn't resist when son and grandson bundled him from the room. Above his objections, I heard the telephone ring in the hall. A minute later, the maid came through to tell me there was a call for me, so I followed her out, glad to be away from the family conflict.

'Audrey? It's very late, is everything all right?'

'Oh, James, thank heavens I've caught you. There's a man. Outside.'

'A man? What's he doing? Hang on, don't answer that. Have you locked the doors?'

'I'd already done it when I saw him. I was just going to bed. I put out the bedroom light and peeked through the blackout curtains like I do every night. He was just standing there, across the road, staring at the house.'

I asked if she could see what he looked like.

'I couldn't make out his face, only his hair.'

'His hair?'

'That's how I spotted him. It's pitch black outside with no streetlights, but I caught a glimpse of a white patch which isn't normally there. I stared for so long my eyes got used to the dark and I could make out his shape. Tall and thin. Then he must have seen me. He looked up, pointed and mouthed a few words. I almost screamed. James, you must come. I'm so frightened.'

'I think he'll be long gone before I'd get there, Audrey. Go round and double check all the doors and windows, then phone the police. I know who he is, and I'll have him picked up.'

She protested, but I insisted she do as I asked and told her I'd speak to her the next morning.

When we'd hung up, I rang Bob Moore. He wasn't there, so I explained to the duty sergeant and asked him to send a constable round to Audrey's house, and to have Stephen Grainger arrested, who should be put in the cells overnight.

I'd barely finished when Alec came down the stairs, and we both went through to the drawing room. He was still breathing heavily when he re-took his seat.

'All I can do is apologise, James. That man would try the patience of a saint sometimes. I don't know what I've done to deserve all of his bad humour tonight. I think the poor fellow gets so frustrated confined to his room most of the time, he feels the need to be obnoxious when he comes out. Makes him feel alive, I suppose.'

I told Alec I thought he'd done very well not to react sooner, and that even I'd bitten my tongue several times, so I wasn't surprised he'd reacted in the end.

'I just have to ignore him, mostly, and try to stop him from drinking, but you can see how mean he can be when he feels like it. He comes up with that nonsense about me being no son of his when he really wants to wind me up.'

'But why would he say such a thing?'

'I think he was about to say I'm a wastrel, that's his usual accusation. My father can't accept his son doesn't share the same passion for the engineering business as he does. He also believes I'm not very good at it and I don't have his acumen.'

'Can I ask you a question about him?'

'Feel free.'

'Would he have known Ellen, Henry Dyer's mother?'

He looked at me for a moment, then shook his head. 'Not that I'm aware of. Why?'

'Oh, nothing. I just wondered. Leamington's such a small town I imagined everyone knows everyone else. A bit like Kenilworth, where I lived.'

'It is a bit like that, but I never heard him mention her.'

I let it go there, because there was nowhere I could take it. We talked for another few minutes until Andrew returned and told us his grandfather had settled. This gave me the opportunity to say I wanted to get to bed too and wished them goodnight.

Upstairs, I lay in the dark, reliving arguments I'd had with my own father, as bitter and pointless as the one I'd witnessed that evening.

TWENTY-FIVE

Tuesday 6th August, 1940

The night was warm and my room stifling, despite an open window. The heat and a whirlwind of thoughts about the Kendricks' relationship, my future with Rachel, Audrey's telephone call, and the puzzle around Henry's murder, kept me awake long into the night. Even after I nodded off in the early hours, I woke sporadically until I could stand it no longer, so I got up at six and sat at the kitchen table, looking out onto the garden, already alive with birds and flying insects. In front of me was my notepad and several sheets of blank paper.

I transferred what I considered to be significant facts onto three sheets in different combinations. So far, I had three suspects: Sebastian Clark, Stephen Grainger and Derek Taylor, all with alibis which, on the face of it, stood up to scrutiny. I added Terry Gleeson and a "Mr Unknown" into the mix, just in case. Under their names I added motive, opportunity, evidence and alibi. I continually came up against a brick wall against one or other of these headings, leading me to scribble questions on a fourth sheet. I'd need to share these with Bob Moore, if only to get the manpower to break down the barriers.

After about thirty minutes, I was still writing when my pen ran out of ink. I cursed and went upstairs to refill it, only to discover I'd not packed a bottle when I'd left my father's. I poked around the bedroom and found none in any of the drawers, so I wandered downstairs again, hoping I'd find some in the bureau I'd seen the night before in the drawing room.

From the hall I could now hear the chink of crockery towards the back of the house and followed the sound to the kitchen, thinking it may be Alec or Andrew, who'd put me right for ink. They weren't there but the maid, washing dishes from the previous night, jumped when I coughed at the doorway.

'Good heavens, sir, you gave me a fright. Is there something you need?'

'A cup of tea would be wonderful, Clarrie, if there's a chance.'

'I'll get you one straight away, sir.' The young woman lifted a small pot from the stove and poured my drink, laying the cup and saucer on the table. 'Will there be anything else, sir?'

'No, thank you. I think I'll find what I need in the drawing room but, if not, I'll come and find you again.'

The bureau wasn't locked, and several pigeonholes held paper, though there was no ink bottle in view. On either side were columns of three drawers, and I found what I was looking for in the bottom one on the right. Alongside it, the white face of a pocket watch caught my eye. The timepiece looked good quality, though no more than I would have expected for a man of Alec Kendrick's position, and I wondered why it had been tucked away in a drawer. I lifted it, wound it, and held it to my ear to see if it worked. The rhythmic tick-tock confirmed it did. When I turned it over to look at the back, the words engraved there told me all I needed to know. I placed the ink bottle back where I'd found it and pocketed the watch. It was only then that I saw the black cover of a notebook. Minutes later, after I'd flicked through its pages, I made a whispered call from the telephone in the hall.

When I returned to the kitchen, Clarrie had left, and the table was now laid with everything for her to prepare breakfast when the household was up. I took a seat and sipped my now-tepid tea. Alec appeared within a couple of minutes.

'Good morning, James. You're up early. Warm night, wasn't it?'

'It was. I hope it's all right, but I got up early and your maid sorted me out a cup of tea.'

'That's not a problem. Make yourself at home.' He made himself a fresh pot then sat opposite me. 'I love it here in the morning, James, before the house starts moving through the day. Somehow it's more homely than our dining room. I think I'd have all my meals in here if the others would let me.'

'You're lucky to have such a fine house, Alec. It can't be easy to keep up.'

I glanced at the clock, then struggled through small talk about the weather and his business until the maid came in and shooed us through to the dining room. The results of my telephone call would take a little time to come to fruition.

Andrew joined us, and we ate a better breakfast than might have been expected on rations, confirming that the well-off aren't as inhibited by such restrictions as the rest of us. Alec and I were left alone when his son set off for work. Soon afterwards, Alec pushed back his chair.

'I'm sorry, James, I have to leave you too. I'll try to pop back at lunchtime, but ask Clarrie for anything you might need.'

I checked the time again. If Kendrick planned to leave, it might be now or never.

'May I ask you a question before you go? It's been puzzling me all morning.'

'Fire away.'

'You've lived here a long time?'

'Ever since I was fifteen. My father bought the place when the business became established. It's far too big, but I expect he wanted to show off.'

'And how long ago did you meet Henry?'

He pursed his lips and scratched his chin. 'Only in the last couple of years. After he retired, certainly.'

'Would he come to the house often?'

'Henry? I don't think he was ever here. We always met at the golf club, or we might have a bite to eat in town. Why do you ask?'

'It's just that, as I told you, I was up early, and I needed some ink because my pen had run out. I know it was a bit of a cheek, but I had a root around in your bureau to see if you had any.'

Kendrick stiffened. I pulled Henry's watch from my pocket and laid it on the table.

'I just wondered why you might have his retirement present tucked away in a drawer, that's all. Alongside Ernest Parkes's notebook.'

For an older man, Kendrick was quick and strong. He leapt round the table and dived towards me, knocking me and my chair to the ground, then knelt on my bad leg with all his weight. I yelped and struggled to push him away, but he'd knocked the wind from me. In seconds, his fingers gripped my throat. He lifted my head to smash it to the ground. Before he could do so, a shout erupted from behind.

'Mr Kendrick!' The maid stood in the doorway, open-mouthed.

Her call distracted her boss long enough for me to roll away, bracing for another attack. Instead, Kendrick jumped to his feet, scrambled across the room, and dashed out of the back door. I shouted to Clarrie to telephone the police, then hobbled after Kendrick. He'd escaped the garden before I reached it, having taken the shortest route down the side to the street. When I reached the front of the house, Kendrick was face-down on the ground, with Terry Gleeson holding the man's arm up his back.

I slumped against the wall, regaining my breath. At that moment, a police car screeched into the road, bell ringing and blue lights flashing. When it stopped at the gate, I was relieved to see two decent-sized coppers climb out, truncheons at the ready.

Alec Kendrick sat on one side of the interview room table, me and Bob Moore on the other.

Half an hour earlier, I'd been in Kendrick's place, passing everything I knew on to Bob. He'd phoned his boss when he'd heard we were on our way into the station with Kendrick, and they'd agreed I'd be allowed temporary status as Inspector in the Special Constabulary. Bob had congratulated me and issued a warrant card. He told me he'd spoken to Grainger, who'd said his appearance at Audrey's had been to apologise and he hadn't meant to scare her. He'd been released, with a warning to stay away from her in future.

We'd agreed I'd sit in on Alec Kendrick's interview. Bob had earlier admitted he'd never handled a murder enquiry, so it was clear he wanted my experience. He kicked off the questioning with the usual confirmation of name, address and other personal details. He indicated for me to take over.

'So, Alec, do you want to tell us what happened?'

'Not without a solicitor.'

'We can get your man down here in no time, if you really want him, but I'm not sure you do. Not yet, anyway — plenty of time for that later. You're not going to deny you know something about Henry Dyer's murder now, are you?'

'I know what you told me, and no more.'

'Then why did you have his watch in your house?'

Kendrick pressed his hands to his face, fingertips covering his eyelids, and exhaled deeply. He then gave a grim laugh and looked me in the eyes. 'You know, James, I can't do this. It runs counter to everything I believe. I'll tell you the truth.'

I'd half-expected he'd react this way. All that I'd heard about Alec Kendrick was that he was a good man. A pillar of his church, a doer of good works. He'd even let off an employee who might have stolen from him and put his business in jeopardy. All he needed was a nudge and he'd come clean.

'I'm guessing you didn't set out to kill Henry.'

'Not for one minute. He'd been a good friend. As you know, we met at the golf club and hit it off straight away. We began playing a round together most weeks, sharing the honours, then we would have lunch either in the clubhouse or at a place on The Parade. I suppose I shouldn't have been taking time away from the factory, since it's been struggling so much, but I needed to get away from it occasionally.'

'I thought the firm was doing well?'

'Not as well as it needed to. We had a few orders coming in, but not enough. My father's right: I don't have his flair for business. Without some quick cash, we'll go under within six months.'

'When did you discover you and Henry were related?'

'What ... how did you know?'

'That painting in your hall is a bit of a giveaway, though I didn't see it at first. I didn't spot the likeness when I met the two of you together, at least no more than any two men of your age. It was only when your father made his outburst, and

I looked at you and Andrew, that the penny dropped how strong your resemblance was to Henry. I'd recognised in the portrait and in her photograph the same family features.' I lay the letter Audrey had found in front of Kendrick. 'What do you know of this?'

He picked it up and read it, his face puzzled until he saw the signature. 'I've never seen it before.'

'That's as may be, but it suggests Henry was your brother.'

'Half-brother.'

'Which I imagine explains the watch. You took it, along with his wallet, to make it look like he'd been robbed, but then couldn't bear to part with the memento. Am I right?'

Bob Moore glanced at me, grinned, shook his head, then addressed Kendrick. 'Is he?'

Kendrick nodded. 'Exactly right.'

'So tell us, Mr Kendrick, how long have you known?'

'Just a few months. Father and I had been arguing one night and I'd bundled him off to bed. He'd been drinking and continuing with his "no son of mine" routine, which he'd only started recently. I told him I *was* his son, the only one he'd got, and he laughed in my face, saying he'd never wanted me and had been forced into taking me on. God forgive me, but I could have struck him. But I didn't. Instead, I demanded he explain. He spilled out the whole venomous story.

'It seems Ellen, Henry's mother, was in service with my parents when she was young. My father forced his attentions on her, and the poor woman became pregnant. Sometime earlier, the woman I'd always thought of as my mother had found she couldn't have children. Her wish for a family, and his guilt, led them to offer to take in the child — me — and bring it up as their own.

'Ellen left their employment soon after I arrived discreetly at a nursing home in the country, and my parents paid her an allowance as recompense.'

I interrupted. 'That's the contract in the letter sent to Ellen?'

'I expect so. As I understand it, she married Henry's father the following year and Henry came along soon afterwards.' He nodded towards the letter. 'It looks like her marriage nullified the arrangement. I suppose Father thought she'd not need the financial support if she had a husband.'

'After you met Henry, did you tell him?'

'Not immediately. I had to pluck up the courage. It was only after your first visit that I got round to doing it. When I did, it was with no other intention than to make the bond with a new member of my family. I even wanted to go and see Henry's mother … my mother … but I thought I should talk to him first.'

'So what went wrong, Alec?'

'You have to believe me when I say I never intended to kill him. When I told him the story, Henry appeared shocked at first, as though he couldn't take it in, then he telephoned me to say he was pleased we'd discovered the truth. But he didn't want it to be public, not while his mother was alive. I didn't want to cause any embarrassment, so I agreed it would be our secret.'

'Then she died. Did Henry still refuse to acknowledge your relationship?'

'No. He didn't have the chance. I asked to meet him on his morning walk. When I got there, he greeted me as I'd hoped he would — as a brother.'

'So why kill him?'

'That day, in the park, he seemed in such good humour I took the chance of asking if he'd consider passing over half our mother's estate. I explained my business was in dire financial straits and I faced ruin, but he refused. My father doesn't know, but I've raided all his savings. We'd have lost the factory, the house and everything to keep us going. I begged and pleaded with Henry. He wouldn't budge. I told him he'd have to hand it over if I took him to court, and Henry's look of disgust before he turned to walk away made me snap. Next minute he was down on the ground, not breathing, with me holding a rock in my hand.'

'Then you panicked and ran away.'

'My first impulse was to confess to the police. Instead, when I'd taken stock, I went to church and confessed to my maker. Nothing would have been gained with me in prison. My business would still shut down with all those men out of work, and my father and son would be penniless.'

'So, it was all a terrible accident? What about Ernest Parkes? Was his death an accident too?'

Kendrick paused before answering. 'In a way, yes. Parkes had discovered I'd been leaking the new designs to competitors. It was the only way I could see of getting the cash we needed to survive. He came and challenged me. When everyone else left for the day, I went down to the factory to plead with him. In my frustration, I shook his ladder and he fell. I checked he wasn't breathing then slipped away.'

I stood and folded my arms. 'You're going to need that solicitor now, Alec. In both cases, if you'd gone with your instinct to confess before being found out, it would have been easier to claim manslaughter. When you hid what you'd done, it became murder. I'm afraid you'll hang for it.'

Without waiting further, Bob started on the paperwork. As the policeman's pen scratched, Kendrick began sobbing his way through a prayer.

It wasn't often I'd witness a murderer with real remorse for what they'd done. Often, the only sorrow they demonstrated was that they'd been caught. Alec Kendrick was different. Even though he'd tried to cover up his crimes, I could see the guilt had been eating away at a decent man who'd made a terrible mistake.

By the time we'd processed Alec Kendrick's arrest and charges, and written all the reports, it was late. With him locked away for the night, and perhaps a good while longer, I was short of a bed for the third time in a week.

I rang Audrey and told her that Henry's murderer was now behind bars. I also begged a room for the night, which she offered gladly, though she sounded surprised I wasn't going home to my wife.

She quizzed me again about Rachel when I arrived at the house, so I lied that it had been a long day and I didn't fancy the train.

'There's also a couple of things I need to sort out over here, so I'll be in Leamington longer than tonight.'

'You're welcome to stay here if you wish, James. I'm glad of the company.'

'Just the one night will be fine, thanks, Audrey, I'll arrange for a B&B after that. I'll be coming and going at all hours, so I think it best to go where I'm not disturbing anyone.'

'Well, if you change your mind, you only have to say and there's a room here for you. It's the least I can do.'

I filled her in on the details of Kendrick's arrest and his reasons. She wept, unable to believe that Henry's friend — and half-brother — had been his killer. Later, Audrey went to finish preparing the evening meal, and I made a telephone call to my father. I asked how he and Mama were, but he sounded distant.

'Can I apologise, Papa?'

'You can, but I'm not sure I'll accept it, Jacob.'

'Then, I'm sorry. I can say no more but believe me, I am. Now this business has finished, I hope I can get back to normal.'

'Are you coming home tomorrow, then?'

'I think I'll need another few days to think about Rachel and me, and where I'm going to live. I can't come back to your house. There's no room.'

The line went quiet for a few seconds.

'Papa?'

'She came round last night — Rachel. I don't know if I should say, but she was crying and told your mama she was missing you. Can't you just come back to her and see where it goes?'

'I don't think so. Rachel's the one who has to decide. I'd be home like a shot if I thought she wasn't going to throw me out again. If I take another day or so to think it through, we might reach something that works. If you see her again, tell her I'll phone soon.'

My father was far from happy, but Audrey called me through to eat, so I asked him to be patient, and gave him the details of where I'd be staying. I also asked if I could see him when I got back to Birmingham. In reply, he spoke gently.

'At times like this, Jacob, there are only two places to look. Inside your heart, and upwards to God. Say a prayer or two, and you'll know what to do.'

Audrey went to bed early, saying she had a headache, and left me thinking through my day. Something nagged at me. Why would Alec Kendrick sell his own secret designs then ask me to investigate? Henry had told him I was good at my job, so he wouldn't have thought I'd bungle it. Then it came to me. I *had* bungled it.

A quick telephone call and fifteen minutes later I walked into Bob Moore's office again. Ten minutes after that, we were on the Kendricks' doorstep.

TWENTY-SEVEN

Wednesday 7th August, 1940

Bob wanted me in again the next morning to tidy the loose ends, and to check he'd not missed any of the procedures required to make a murder charge stick. He looked done in.

'Were you at it all night, Bob?'

'Andrew Kendrick cracked at about two.' He waved at the papers spread across his desk. 'Then there was this lot to write up. At first the lad denied all knowledge, until I pointed out his father had admitted to the killings and would hang. I left him to stew on it, and when I went back, he did the right thing. His story was much the same as Alec Kendrick's had been, except, of course, it was Andrew who'd stolen and sold the documents. The father only found out about this later, after Henry Dyer had been murdered.'

'And it was Andrew who met Henry in the park, and lashed out when he wouldn't bail out the business?'

'That's right. He'd overheard the argument between his father and grandfather, so he knew Henry was Alec's half-brother. He contacted Henry allegedly to introduce himself. Didn't you suspect him at all, James?'

'Not really. Now I think back, there are things I might have seen. The designs were signed out with an initial which I took as Alec's, but it was Andrew's. Everyone said Parkes's death was an accident, even the coroner, and it seemed so unlikely the thefts would be carried out by a family member, I never even bothered to look. The comment Andrew made to me on a trip out, about brothers needing to look after each other, also makes sense with hindsight.'

There seemed to be no point dredging through the missed hints any further, and we turned our attention to checking through his reports. When we'd done it twice, we pulled in his desk sergeant to go through them again, just to be sure. Bob then released Alec Kendrick with a warning that he may face charges for his false confession.

We'd finished by mid-morning, and Bob directed me to a couple of lodgings I might try, where they let rooms on a weekly basis. I wandered round to look at them with little enthusiasm. None of them would be a permanent home, so in many ways it didn't matter. As long as I had a roof over my head and a bed I could afford, not too far out of town, I wouldn't mind until I either made it up with Rachel or found a place of my own. I chose the second one I looked at. The owners seemed a bit more friendly and had a telephone for use in emergencies.

I put away my few things, went to the town market to buy essentials I'd not brought with me, and wandered round, wondering if I should call Rachel. The first telephone box I found wasn't working, and the next was occupied, with two men waiting, so I decided the omens were against a good outcome from a conversation with my wife. Instead, I looked for a café, feeling like something stronger but knowing I shouldn't drink. I went into the first one that had a spare table.

Inside, with a tepid cup of tea, a curly-edged cheese sandwich, and a stained tablecloth, I thought about my options. In the space of a week, I'd lost my wife and my home, and I wasn't even sure I had a job with my father any longer. Even if I did, there was no way I could do it travelling from Leamington every day, and the prospect of moving back in with him sent shivers down my spine. In my early life I'd worked at sea, so not much future for that in landlocked Warwickshire. I'd picked fruit, farmed a little, and been a policeman. I wanted to work in the open fields, but not without Rachel, so Bob Moore's offer was the best on the table. The only real problem was, I didn't want to do it. And I was pretty sure I'd never get my wife back if I accepted.

After half an hour nursing my drink, getting nowhere and with increasingly dirty looks from the café owner, I walked back to my lodgings. I lay on the bed and stared at the ceiling for ages, unable to either undress and climb under the covers or shake myself into anything more productive than writing a long apology to Alfie Wilson. At half past five, I dragged myself downstairs for an almost inedible evening meal of gristle, undercooked potatoes, and watery cabbage. When I pushed it away unfinished, the landlady made a comment about there being a war on, and said I should be grateful for anything she could manage with the rations she received. I apologised and left.

The streets were quiet and the evening muggy, making every step feel like walking through treacle. After I dropped my note through Alfie Wilson's letterbox, I put one foot in front of the other, with no sense of where I was going, until I turned a corner and the railway station appeared across the road. Outside the main entrance was a telephone box.

'Rachel?' I could hardly get the word out when I heard her voice.

'James? Where are you?'

'I'm … I'm still in Leamington.'

'Oh.'

'Didn't Papa tell you?'

'Of course he did, but that was yesterday. I thought you might be back in Birmingham now.'

'Can I come home, then?'

The line went quiet, so I knew the answer before she gave it. Her voice was softer when she did.

'I don't think so. Not yet. How am I to know you'll not just start another case when your new policeman friend asks you to?'

'I won't, I promise.'

'Well, we'll have to see, won't we? I want you back, I really do, but not if you're putting yourself in harm's way all the time. Give it a couple of weeks, then come and visit.'

'But, Rachel —'

'No buts, James. That's the way it has to be.'

At breakfast, the chatter was all about the bombs dropped on the south of England the previous night. A car backfired just beyond the dining-room window and an elderly lady almost jumped out of her skin.

I'd spent the entire evening trying to figure out how my life would be without Rachel. We'd married late, and I had plenty of self-sufficiency behind me, but I'd become used to the love she gave me. Over our last year, I'd painted pictures in my head of our lives together, stretching away into old age. And now that was being replaced by a blank canvas again.

I buttered another slice of toast, thinly, preserving the landlady's hard-won rations. The salesman sharing my table asked me if I'd be in town long.

'I'm not sure. I'd planned to leave in the next day or so, but now I find I may be here for a while.' I looked around the room. 'Though I'll need to find a place of my own. I can't afford to stay here too long.'

'Funny you should say that, mate. Customer of mine asked me yesterday if I knew anyone who wanted a place. He has two cottages on the edge of Leamington — he's trying to get tenants in.'

'Do they have any land with them?'

'Couldn't say. Didn't take much notice, to tell you the truth. I'm away to Coventry tomorrow, so I didn't think I'd bump into anyone interested.' He took a notebook and pen from his jacket pocket and scribbled a few words, then tore out the page. 'Here, these are his details. Give him a call.'

An hour later, I'd trudged out to the first of the cottages, the ache in my leg setting my teeth on edge. I wasn't in the mood, but I didn't like it anyway. The owner, Mr Speedwell, didn't seem to mind and gave me a ride to his second property. This, like the first, had no land and the tiniest of gardens, but I decided it would do for a few weeks. Speedwell's smile disappeared when he heard I was looking for work, and told me to come back to see him when I had some. I told him the rent wouldn't be a problem.

'You say that now, Mr Given, and, sure enough, it might be fine for a few weeks. But what if you don't find a job, or find one that doesn't pay very much? What will happen to my rent then, eh? Before we know it, you'll be owing me big time, and I'll end up out of pocket. No, no. As I say, come and see me when you're settled with something.'

He didn't bother to give me a lift back, and I had to limp, as best I could, down streets I didn't know, trying to find the way to my digs. At least twice I went astray and needed to double back. On the edge of the town centre, I plonked down on a low wall outside a pub and rubbed my aching thigh, cursing Speedwell, the Kendricks, my father, and even Rachel, who, between them, had put me where I was.

Laughter and the sound of a piano seeped from the pub onto the street, and I cursed some more. Then it began to rain.

It must have been nine o'clock when I fell through the front door of my lodgings, barely able to stand. My collision with the hall table, and the clattering of my keys on the tiles, brought my landlady, Mrs Tamar, from the comfort of her front room.

'Mr Given!'

I let out what could only be described as a cackle, and she shouted for her husband. He dashed out and took me by the arm.

'Come on, sir. Let's get you up to bed.'

'It's Rachel — she's my wife, you know — she threw me out. Me! And all I was doing was helping a friend.'

At least that's what I thought I'd said, though it probably didn't come out like that. The response I got was an exasperated tut from Mrs Tamar and a clear instruction I was to move out the next day.

'I can't be having my guests coming home in this state, Mr Given. This is a respectable establishment. I don't mind a gentleman taking a glass, but this is too much.'

Having issued her decree, she went inside and left her husband to put me to bed.

TWENTY-EIGHT

Friday 9th August, 1940

Banging on the door woke me. It was still dark. A man's voice, shouting.

'Mr Given, wake up. There's a telephone call. Urgent.'

Despite my throbbing head I bounced past Mr Tamar and took the stairs two at a time. In the hallway, where the grandfather clock told me it was still a few minutes before five, the landlady passed me the receiver. 'He says he's your father, love. Hope everything is all right.'

She remained leaning against the wall, a cigarette hanging from her bottom lip. I raised an eyebrow and nodded towards the door, but she stayed, arms folded.

'Papa? What's wrong?'

'Jacob? Haven't you heard?'

'Heard what? I've been asleep.'

'The bombing.'

Any remaining tiredness disappeared. 'Bombing?' The landlady's eyes widened at the word. 'In Birmingham? Are you all right?'

'Yes, yes, we're all fine, Rachel too. A German plane came over in the night and dropped bombs on Erdington. They're saying it was aiming for the aircraft factory but missed. We think a man was killed.'

'But the family is safe?'

'Mama is terrified. We felt the explosions; the whole house rattled. Then we didn't sleep. Even I was worried we might be next.'

He begged me to return to Birmingham. I told him I'd speak to Rachel, then we'd take it from there. I promised to catch a train later in the morning. When I'd hung up, I explained about the air raid to the landlady, though she'd heard enough to guess what had happened, so I asked if I could telephone my wife.

'Of course, love. You make as many calls as you like. We have to stick together in times like this.' She nodded at an incongruous brown teapot on the hall table. 'You just leave the money in there when you're done.'

It took a couple of minutes for the operator to answer, with an apology that they were very busy, then a few minutes more to be put through to Rachel.

'James, thank God you've called.'

No silence, no recrimination. Just relief following a night where the war had caught up with us.

'Please tell me you're safe.'

'For now. It's been frightening. And so close. All week we've had sirens, then tonight we heard the explosions. After that, I lay awake in the dark listening for more, so scared. When I looked out, all our neighbours were on the street, watching the sky. Please, James…'

'What?'

'Please come home. I need you.'

I told her I'd be on the first train back.

I threw on my clothes and stuffed my few things into my case, then almost ran to the station, despite the searing pains in my leg and head. I might as well have taken my time. The first train north wasn't due until quarter to seven and the platform was already packed with people, like me, trying to reach their loved ones in Birmingham. The stationmaster and his staff were trying to bring some semblance of order, but it was clear there'd be serious delays. Not everyone would manage to get onto the first, or even the second, train. I tried showing my brand-new warrant card, but the man in charge was having none of it.

'Sorry, sir, but you're all in the same boat. If I start doing favours, I'll have a riot on my hands, and you wouldn't want that, would you?'

All I could do was apologise and try to find a seat to wait, though even these were few and far between. The train arrived half an hour late, already packed to the doors, and left a full hour after the scheduled time, without me on it. Someone made an announcement over the loudspeakers that the second train had been cancelled, but the next one would have extra carriages. By the time it arrived at eleven o'clock, tempers were frayed, children were crying and it had started to rain. Within minutes, the mass had cleared the platform and somehow squeezed onto the train.

A cheer went up when we rolled out of the station, only to turn to a collective groan when we stopped again, half a mile up the track. A conductor pushed into my carriage and explained to passengers that this was the way it would be all the way to Birmingham, where there had been damage close to one of the railway lines. This had wreaked havoc with the timetables, with trains getting in and out of the city as best they could.

By the time we pulled into Moor Street Station at one o'clock, my stomach was complaining that I hadn't eaten since the previous night, but I couldn't stop. Rachel would be frantic that I hadn't arrived when I'd said I would. No taxis were to be had outside the station, and the queues at the bus stops showed they'd been affected as badly as the railway.

Though in no mood nor state to walk the mile home, I had no option, and my leg throbbed for the entire journey. I stopped at our gate to catch my breath for a few seconds and to run through my prepared speech one more time.

The trek from Leamington had provided plenty of time to rehearse what I wanted to say to Rachel. I'd apologise, but not so much as to suggest I regretted having looked for Henry's murderer. The only thing I regretted was that it had caused her so much worry about the danger to me, though I would do the same again if I thought I could help, regardless of the risk. I'd say that if the air raid of the previous night had taught us anything, it had shown that danger was everywhere — even in our beds, death could drop from the sky. It had also shown us we needed to be close to the ones we loved, and stupid squabbles meant nothing. I'd leave her in no doubt she was the only one for me, and I'd never willingly leave her again.

With what I hoped would be the right words on my lips, I pushed my key into the front door. As it swung inwards, Rachel rushed down the hall and flung her arms around my neck. There was no need for my speech.

We spent the afternoon trying to get back to where we used to be. We talked about her fears for me, and I promised to try to avoid getting mixed up in things that didn't concern me. I said I needed to get out of the city, back to a life in the open air, and Rachel agreed we should try. By evening, we'd made our peace.

After our meal, we walked to a post-box to return my warrant card to Bob Moore, then sat close together on our settee, listening to wireless reports of the air raids that had taken place the previous night. London and the south had borne the brunt of the attacks again, with the one on Birmingham being the only one in the Midlands, leading us to think it might just have been a practice run — there'd be more to come. Even though we turned the dial to a music programme after a while, this thought kept me awake into the small hours.

On Monday, I arrived at the workshop early, knowing there'd be a pile of paperwork to catch up on, and I wasn't mistaken. My father, perfectly capable of dealing with the business side, but always reluctant, had stepped further and further back since I'd been with him. Now he'd only had to deal with the most urgent items in my absence. When he came down, he nodded in my direction, then began measuring the cloth on his table. He wasn't about to come to me, so I left it until dinnertime to go to him.

'Can we talk, Papa?'

'Of course, Jacob. Take a seat.'

'Not here. Somewhere comfortable.' I looked around. 'And private.'

'I'm busy, but if that is what you want, come upstairs later. We'll go in the parlour.'

After work, my mother fussed and I chatted with Sarah, Meena, Anna and my Aunt Miriam for a while, all wanting every detail of what I'd been up to in Leamington, until I was able to escape to my father's hideaway. We sat on armchairs either side of the dead fireplace, and I was about to speak when he held up a hand to stop me.

'Let me go first please, Jacob … James.'

This was the first time he'd ever acknowledged my change of name. The shock must have shown on my face.

'I know, son. It's such a big item for both of us, how you wish to be called. For me, you've seemed to want to lose all of our family's history, everything our people have suffered over the centuries. For you, it's how you see yourself. Not Russian, not happily Jewish, but an Englishman. If it is what you want, then I should try to respect your wishes. I should also respect your wishes when it comes to where you want to work.'

'Papa —'

'No, James, let me finish. It's taken a long time for me to say these things. I've always known you didn't want to follow in my footsteps but, believe me, I thought it would be better if you did. It is steady, and it is safe. Working in the fields can't guarantee an income from one week to the next, and policemen end up injured or dead all the time. Even you. A ruined leg, and almost killed last year. Believe me, tailoring is a much better idea.' He grinned and placed a hand on my knee. 'But that isn't you, is it? You need to be outside or putting the world to rights. Just like Ariel.'

His mention of my brother's name took away the closeness I'd been beginning to feel. 'You were always so proud of him, Papa.'

'I've always been proud of all of you.'

'But Ariel the most.'

My father looked puzzled. 'Is that how it has seemed to you, James?'

'Always. He didn't become a tailor, but when he joined the army you bragged about him for weeks. When he went to Spain, you thought him a hero. When I joined the police, you hardly noticed. No photograph in my uniform, no parading me in front of your friends, nothing.'

He didn't speak but went to his small sideboard and lifted out a bottle of brandy and a glass. He pulled a face and rubbed his left rib before turning to me. 'You won't have one?'

I shook my head. He poured a drop and smelled it.

'I shouldn't either, not before eating. But I think I need it. You have it wrong, son. Ariel was my first boy, and the things he did were new to me, so they were special. But not above you, or Sarah, or Eli. When you became a policeman I could have burst with pride, but we hardly spoke then, and I couldn't tell you. My friends knew, even if you didn't. You've been a good man, in ways I could never be. Protecting people, keeping the law. Good things.' He took a taste, walked over to me and took my hand, pulling me to my feet. For the next few minutes we hugged, and he repeated, over and over, 'James, James, my son.'

The telephone call came at ten o'clock, just before Rachel and I went to bed.

It was my cousin, Anna.

'James, it's your father. I'm so, so sorry.'

EPILOGUE

It only took a short time for Andrew Kendrick's case to be heard at Warwick Assizes. The murder of a former police superintendent had accelerated it, as had young Kendrick's confession and his promise of a guilty plea. While I waited for my turn in the court, I read depressing reports in the *Daily Post* of heavy bombing throughout the Midlands on the previous night. To keep the Nazis in the dark, as if they wouldn't know where they'd raided, no towns were mentioned, but I knew Birmingham had been hit badly. In contrast, stories of attacks on the enemy listed Turin and Milan, as well as the location of every aerodrome and other target across Germany. I found the news of such carnage equally sad. After a few more pages of the same, I came to the financial pages and my eyes glazed over.

I put down my newspaper and popped my head into the courtroom. The space, small, octagonal and high-ceilinged, with the judge on his oversized, red leather seat towering over the proceedings, was both cosy and intimidating. Andrew Kendrick looked small and vulnerable under his gaze. The defendant's barrister was on his feet. It sounded as if his client had pleaded guilty, as he'd said he would, and a case was being made for leniency. I'd not now be called as a witness, so I slipped back outside, and didn't wait to hear the result.

A week after the trial, and a month after my father's funeral, I arrived home and went through to the kitchen to put my arms round Rachel's waist as she stood at the sink.

'I have good news. Well, great news really. Zac Bloom has agreed to take over as manager. He came to see me today, said he'd thought about my offer and decided he'd take it.'

Rachel turned and hung herself around my neck. 'Are you sure he can do it?'

'Oh yes, he worked with Papa for years and knows every inch of the trade. He'll have no problems with the business.'

'So, what does it mean?'

'Well, most importantly, it will keep an income for Mama. Zac is experienced but young enough to have the energy my father had lost. If I'm not there, then my wages will more than cover the extra he'll be paid, and even leave a little to invest in the business.'

'Then if you intend on being unemployed and fancy-free, you'd better open the letter which came today.' She lifted an envelope from the table and wafted it in front of my face. 'It's got a Kenilworth postmark, James. This could be what we've been waiting for.'

Sure enough, it had come from Mrs Harris, the woman whose house we'd viewed on the day of our coach trip. It seemed so long ago.

I opened the letter. 'She says she's happy to accept our offer, and she's convinced her neighbour to give us the option to buy two extra acres of land.'

I'd never heard Rachel let out such a scream as she did at that moment.

'When does she say we can move in?'

'Within the month.'

A NOTE TO THE READER

Dear Reader,

I hope you've enjoyed *A Malignant Death*, or if you're only flicking through before you start, I hope you do enjoy it. I enjoyed writing it.

One thing which fascinated me as I researched the places and times of the James Given novels was how there can be a degree of normality when a war is imminent, or even underway. Echoes of this persist even in our current period of history. In late 1939 and early- to mid-1940, defence preparations were in place in Britain, but air bombardment was limited, with the first casualties on the mainland not being recorded until late-May 1940. As a result, people went about their normal lives and although men of fighting age were being conscripted, many jobs were exempt. Later, of course, the horrors of war became a reality for most people, up and down Britain, but, as far as I have read, these early days were different. It is in this world that *A Malignant Death* is set. A world in which the killing of one person was still of note.

The title, as with all the James Given series, is from William Shakespeare. This time it is from *Richard III* and if you've finished the book, you'll understand the reference.

I love to hear from readers, so please contact me through my **Facebook page** or send me a message through **Twitter**. You can also see my latest news on **my website** and sign up for notifications. Reviews are so important to authors, and if you enjoyed the novel I would be grateful if you could spare a few minutes to post a review on **Amazon** and/or **Goodreads**.

Thanks for reading!

Charlie Garratt

Sapere Books is an exciting new publisher of brilliant fiction and popular history.

To find out more about our latest releases and our monthly bargain books visit our website:
saperebooks.com

Printed in Great Britain
by Amazon

19456837R00142